WICKED GIRL

WICKED #3

PIPER LAWSON

Published by Piper Lawson Books

Line and copy editing by Cassie Roberston
Cover by Natasha Snow
Cover photography by Lindee Robinson

1

"Jax." Across the table, Camille Taylor's tongue darts out to brush her lip. "We need to talk."

Everything about her reads indecisive, which undermines the professional look she's got going on. High-neck blouse. Bun like a ballerina.

If she wanted to be a ballerina once, this gig must've been a rude awakening.

"What's the problem?" I ask, impatient, shifting in the padded leather chair and eyeing her up over the desk.

"It's Anne. She's been here a year. But she doesn't seem to be settling in."

Annie's eighth grade homeroom teacher

flicks her gaze toward the classroom door, like my kid can hear her from the hall.

"She's creative. Smart. But she keeps to herself. I don't think she's making many friends. Occasionally she's disruptive."

My shoulders tighten. "Disruptive how."

She hesitates before uttering a string of words I'm sure I've misheard.

"What?" I demand.

"She glued feminine hygiene products to one of her classmate's books."

Shit.

I fight the urge to rip one of my fingernails. They're all pretty much gone anyway.

"Oh, and Jax?"

"Yeah?"

"Is she channeling that creativity into other outlets? She was telling one of the boys in class about your music."

I shake my head. "She swims. She doesn't even listen to my music."

"I find that hard to believe. We don't know everything our children do."

"Annie doesn't keep secrets from me." My jaw tightens.

"Anne's a bright girl. She's got excellent

language and math skills. I wish she'd connect more with the other students—use her abilities more constructively." Her gaze flicks past me, nervous, then back. "I understand from her file she's had some changes recently. That can lead to acting out."

My hands tighten on the armrests. "Tell you what. You do your job and I'll do mine."

I shove out of my chair and cross to the door.

"Annie." Outside, the red head of hair lifts from where she's studying her phone with a pained expression. "Let's go."

We follow the sidewalk out the front of the private school. It's all brick and landscaping, and I wonder again what the money pays for that's so different from the public school I went to. More trees? The lawn gets mowed every week instead of once a month?

I glance over at my kid.

In her school uniform, she looks the same as any other eighth grader in this place. But in the past few years, she's changed.

She wears her hair differently. It used to be in braids and now it's down or in a ponytail, the kind that sticks out of the top of her head.

I hit the locks on the Bentley, and we both shift inside.

I put the car in gear and pull out of the lot. "Miss Taylor says you glued something to some kid's books."

Caramel eyes land on me for the first time all night. "They're called tampons, Jax."

Her lilting voice wraps around each word like she's underlining them.

It barely registers that she calls me by my first name anymore. I curse whatever god exists that it's my job to ask, "Why?"

"She swiped mine from gym last week. So I figured if she needed them so badly, she could have them."

"When did you get your… you know?"

"Period?" She sighs, shifting in the passenger seat to look out the window. "A few months ago. Don't worry. Mom helped me when I saw her at Christmas."

It takes all my control not to swerve.

It's almost April.

I still haven't done anything about the "you're becoming a woman" literature my manager rustled up for me. It's in a locked drawer, next to the stack of cash I'll use for the hit on the misguided kid who asks her to prom in four years.

Four years? Jesus.

Some days I think that if I'd known the custody battle with Grace for my kid would've taken a year of our lives and dragged my sister through the mud—something she blames entirely on me when I drop my kid off for holiday visits—maybe I wouldn't have done it.

But I can't say that. I can't even let myself think it for long or I find myself reaching for a crutch. Because this is what I wanted. Everything I wanted.

If it's not enough, I don't know what I'll do.

I force myself back to the conversation. "She also said you were talking about my work. My music."

The noise sounds like a snort. "That's not your work anymore. You haven't touched a guitar all year. You used to play with Ryan."

"Uncle Ryan."

"The last time he came by was six months ago."

Christ, she notices everything. It doesn't feel like that long since I saw Mace, but her mind's like a damn video recorder.

Outside our house, I hit the button on my visor and the gates swing open. The Bentley cruises up the long drive, past the rows of trees and flower beds someone planted a long time ago.

We live fifteen minutes from the school and she doesn't have any friends close by. For the first time, I wonder why not.

"Annie?"

"Anne."

"*Annie*."

She grinds her teeth next to me. I want to shake her or point out she's living in a damn mansion with everything she could want. And some days, it's as if she doesn't notice.

I take a breath to steady myself as I hit the button for the garage and angle the car inside. "I've never seen you with any friends from school."

"I hang out with Cash and Drew at lunch."

"No girls."

"So?"

"Your teacher thought you might be trying to impress a boy."

She snorts. "Those two are not worth impressing."

"Good." Relief has my shoulders sagging, because if she's into boys, I can't deal with that.

"Do you want to know if I'm a lesbian?"

How I manage to throw the car into park, I'll never know. Especially when every instinct is to hit reverse and mash on the gas pedal of life.

"You're thirteen years old."

"I'll be fourteen in the summer." She opens her door and scrambles out, leaning back in after. "If I do like boys, I wouldn't waste my time on either of them. Drew is smashing Chloe Hastings, and I'm pretty sure Cash doesn't have testicles."

The door slams before I can process those words.

I rub my fingers over the bridge of my nose. There's no way this week could get worse.

Until my phone rings.

2

HALEY

Vinyl.

Computer hardware upgrades.

A great cup of coffee.

Seafood doesn't even make the shortlist of things I'll shell out for.

Though here in Philly, mussels are hauled off boats every day, which means they don't have to be expensive.

This place is expensive.

I reach for the front door, but an attendant dressed in black beats me to it.

The restaurant is cozy, intimate, and definitely not my choosing. A dozen tables sit under fairy lights sprinkled in the ceiling and corners.

A familiar blond man stands abruptly when he spots me across the restaurant.

"Wow. You look gorgeous," Carter says as I pull up in front of the table, his gaze running over me. "This for me?"

I smooth a hand over my skirt. "Actually, I was at Wicked for meetings. If I'm coding, it's yoga pants and coffee stains all the way."

He looks good too. He always does. Tonight he's wearing dress pants and a crisp button-down. His blond hair curls at the collar. Carter rounds the table to drop a kiss on my mouth, and I turn my face. He catches my cheek instead.

Burn, I imagine Serena saying.

The chair is pushed in behind me—maybe by the same ghoulish attendant, because he's gone before I can turn around.

I open the menu. "Food first, then work? I'm starving."

"It's always work with you." His grin is teasing, but he complies. When the server comes, Carter orders a bottle of wine. "How do you like the restaurant?"

"Very *Midsummer Night's Dream*.'" He

chuckles. "How's the tenure application going?"

Carter's brows scrunch together. "It's always hard being the youngest to do something. The administration wants to find reasons to tell you no, or not yet. Of course, I'm not going to let them get away with it."

Our wine is delivered and poured, and Carter orders lobster. I get the steak. Rare.

"You're looking for blood tonight," he observes.

"Maybe a little."

"Wicked's living up to its name, huh?"

I take a sip of my wine, feel it tingle through me as I turn the stem in my fingers. "I didn't realize how hard it would be to convince people of things. Maybe it's my age. Or inexperience. Or the fact that I have a vagina."

"For the record, I love that you have a vagina."

I swallow a laugh. "But sometimes... sometimes I think people just don't like change." Work is a safe subject with Carter, and it feels good to vent to someone other than Serena.

"That's what's perfect about computers,"

Carter says. "It's just you and a terminal, and you can change the world."

He talks a lot about changing the world, but I know he means solving interesting technical problems while making money.

It's not a bad thing; it's just how he is. He likes a certain lifestyle and wants to be well-known. He's brilliant at what he does, so he can afford that desire.

"Sometimes I wonder how things might have been different if I'd gotten back into school. I could be a grad student by now."

"You're one of the best coders I've met, degree or not. You take apart problems like no one I know, because you're genuinely curious about them and you believe you can solve them. And, I'm glad you're not a grad student by now."

I raise a brow.

"If you were my grad student, we couldn't do this." His eyes sparkle.

Our meal arrives. When my steak, potatoes, and carrots are set on the scratchy white tablecloth, I let out a little groan that goes unnoticed by Carter, who's looking at his lobster with both anticipation and satisfaction. We dig in, and the first few bites have me sighing.

Okay, maybe there's more to this nice restaurant thing than I thought.

I look at Carter, happily devouring his lobster, and a memory flashes across my mind. Mace hurling his guts into a bucket after ordering diner lobster. My mouth twitches despite the long day.

"What're you laughing at?" Carter prompts.

"Nothing. Just a memory."

It's shocking how many memories I have of that tour.

Shocking because it was only a month. Not shocking because the human brain records new things a disproportionate amount of the time. And nearly everything I experienced on that tour was new.

Living with musicians and roadies in hotels and on a bus.

Learning how to operate one of the best sound systems in the business.

Falling in love with a man I never should've met.

I mentally slap myself. Usually I catch my brain before it goes down that path. But tonight, whether it's the long day or the wine or the fairy lights, I don't catch it in time.

He's here. Humming along my skin.

The sound of his voice laughing in my ear.

The feel of his lips the first time he kissed me.

The look on his face the day he walked away.

My stomach squeezes, and I reach for more wine.

"Good thing we got a bottle," Carter quips. "Since your mood's already improved, I don't need to show you this. I will anyway." He sets down his fork and knife and lifts his phone. "We have an offer."

He slides his phone in front of me between the dinner plates the waitress set in front of us. I shift in my chair, uncrossing and recrossing my legs to get more comfortable.

The piece of software we've been building is actually our second project together. After we won the competition with my music program Digital Record Enhancement, or DRE (as Serena named it), we decided we made a pretty good team. We turned a version of it into an app that's available on every device to amateur and professional producers and provides a steady, if small, revenue stream.

This new program we want to sell outright to a company that will do the same.

The six-figure number on the screen imprints on my mind.

"Wow. I'm not going to lie. I know where my fifty percent is going," I say.

He raises a brow. "Fifty?"

"That's what we agreed."

"Fine." He grins, and I can't tell if he was just pushing my buttons. One of the reasons I can't quite get a handle on him—and that I never really want to. "Celebrate with me. Come home with me tonight."

I swallow the sigh.

We've done it before. Not enough that I'd call it a pattern, which is why he's not sure of himself when he asks. Carter's intelligent and attractive. And if he's a flake, that's not a crime.

When I'm bored, I can resist. It's when I'm lonely—which takes a lot given my tolerance for being alone—that it's hard to say no.

I never crave sex, but sometimes it feels like I'm desperate for human connection, even if the human in question isn't the one I want to connect with.

The ring of my phone interrupts us.

The number on the screen has my spine stiffening.

I hit Ignore and take a steadying breath as I fix a smile on my face and focus on my dinner companion. "I appreciate the offer, but I have work to do tomorrow."

"You realize how wrong that is? Between your inheritance and this money, you don't have to work at all." I open my mouth to argue, but he does it for me. "Of course, I know you couldn't deal with that. It's not in you not to try new things—to learn all the time."

And that's why I do this. Because even if Carter's never going to be a kindred spirit, he understands what it's like to do the work because you can. Because you want to. Because wasting your abilities is a crime.

The phone rings again, a different tone.

Now, it's a video call.

Of course it is.

He won't stop. I know it as surely as I know the bill will come and Carter will make another play before he puts me in my car and I go home alone.

My gaze flicks around the restaurant as if I'm looking for an escape.

Maybe I am.

No luck.

My body shivers with nerves or anticipation.

I can handle Carter blindfolded. This man, even a thousand miles away and on the phone? This is going to be harder.

I hit Accept.

I've seen Jax Jamieson on TV, but his image now, a little grainy from questionable reception, is something else. Because those eyes are on me, and though it's dark wherever he is and I can't make out their trademark amber color, the shape is the same. His sculpted mouth. The hard jaw. The hair falling over his face.

"Jax." I say his name as coolly as I can. "Can I call you back?"

"No."

I lift my gaze to Carter, apologetic. "Excuse me one moment." I shift out of my chair and duck into the hallway by the coatrack.

"Are you on a date?" His commanding tone has me bristling.

I take in the near-black backdrop. "Are you in a coffin?"

His eyes narrow. "We don't talk in two years and now you're trying to enforce my contract."

"I don't enforce contracts."

"Bullshit. One of your suits threatened me. You're seriously going to take the song I gave you and produce it without me?"

I think of the sheet of paper I've carried around for the better part of three years. "It's not a threat. It's a courtesy. We want to give you notice."

"It's my song," he grinds out. "You can't do whatever the hell you want with it."

"It was a gift," I retort, my voice rising too. "In case you've forgotten, that's how gifts work."

I brace myself for a chain reaction, one detonation leading to another, but Jax surprises me by regaining his composure. "You've changed."

"So have you. We all have, Jax." I take a deep breath, hold it for a count of five, and let it out. “You have a choice. Do the album. Or let someone else finish what you started.”

I hit End without waiting for him to respond.

In the bathroom, I smooth out my appearance and pretend the shortest call in history didn’t shake me to my core before returning to Carter.

“So what do you say?” He grins, all teeth and boyish charm. “Nightcap at my place?”

3

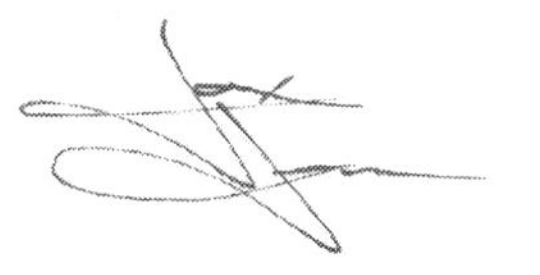

"Burger or nuggets?" I slide my sunglasses down my nose and glance toward the passenger seat.

My daughter pulls out an earbud and looks between me and the drive-through window. "I told you. I'm vegetarian."

I give up and pull out of the lane.

"Why don't you order anything?"

"Huh?"

"You used to get nuggets. You said it was the sweet and sour sauce of the gods."

I'm not telling my kid "because once you turn thirty, it's harder to keep the six-pack they're paying you for."

Which puts us back in a standoff.

The silence is getting to me. I used to be able to take long trips alone. Hell, I craved them.

But the first-class flight from Dallas to Philadelphia and the ride from the airport in my rented Acura has been filled with a quiet tension.

For a moment though, I'm grateful she's in her own world. I soak in the place—my emotions—as I drive through the streets of downtown.

The locals are still dressed in coats and a few boots. The trees are growing leaves. They look hopeful.

That makes one of us.

In the five days since I called Haley, I have run through a dozen responses.

To tell Wicked to fuck off. To ignore them. To unleash my lawyers in that snarling furor only expensive litigators can manage.

In the end, I lay awake staring at the ceiling and remembering the song I wrote. The thought of someone else taking it, making it theirs, and possibly ruining it?

I'm not going to risk it. I need to fix this in person.

We pull up to the valet at the hotel.

"I thought we were getting a house," Annie says, peering out the window and looking up.

"I said I booked the *Rittenhouse*. We have a suite. You'll be home by the summer."

"Everything will have changed in three months. Why couldn't I stay with Mom?"

Because she'd never let me live it down.

"Because you're my kid. I said we were coming to Philly for a while, so that's what we're doing."

My voice is sharp and she blinks at me. For a second I see her, the younger version. Before she wore shiny crap on her mouth and put her hair in strange ponytails.

I miss that version. But as quick as it appeared, it's gone, and the indifference is back.

We get out of the car and the manager greets us. I hand the keys to the valet.

"Mr. Jamieson, it's a pleasure to see you again. And who is this?"

"This is Annie."

I glance back to make sure my daughter is following. Her sullen countenance lurks at my back as Rodney shows us upstairs before handing Annie and me each a keycard.

I open the door to the two-bedroom suite with a view of the park. "You've changed something."

His brows rise. "The carpet and the drapes, Mr. Jamieson."

The joke is on the tip of my tongue, but I stop myself.

"You used to stay here?" Annie asks as he leaves.

It's the first time she's sounded interested, though she's still looking out at the park. I saunter over and stop at her side, taking in the view.

"When we recorded *Redline*. And *Abandon*."

"And now you're recording the fourth. What's it called?"

I hiss out a breath. "It doesn't have a name, because I haven't decided I'm going to do it."

"Why don't you want to?" Annie asks, her gaze sharp.

"That part of my life is over. I chose to come home. To be with you."

"Awesome," she says, like it's really not. When she turns toward me, I expect her to launch into another tirade about our sudden trip, but she says, "My first memory of you was at one of your concerts. On stage, it was like no one could touch you." Tingling runs through my body, not from the memory, but from hearing how she saw me. "You're a different person now."

I drop the curtain and cross the room, setting my phone on the table by the door. "It's on stage where I was different. Now I'm the same person I was before."

Our luggage arrives, and the staff unloads four large suitcases. I slip the guy a fifty.

Annie grabs the handle of one and starts toward the door on the far side of the living room.

"Slow your roll."

She stops and turns, her movements exaggerated. "What."

"Where do you think you're going?"

"Bedroom."

"Not the master."

"It's the least you can do for dragging me here."

I try not to laugh. "You're thirteen. I go, you follow."

She enters the master and takes a look around. She lets out a little sigh at the soaker tub.

If I spoil her, it's natural. I want to make up for everything she's been through. Ten years of living in a dump with a man she never should've called her father. Who Grace never should've called her husband. Now he's serving two years for domestic assault while my sister reclaims her life.

Grace's job as a pharma rep is paying for the house he nearly lost with his drinking and drug habits. Nearly. I had my lawyer work out how to compensate them for some of their bills.

It was the one deal I ever made with her asshole of a spouse.

"So what? You need this for all your preppy shirts?" Annie looks up from the closet.

"I don't have that many preppy shirts." A few years ago, all I owned were T-shirts and hoodies.

Now I do charity auctions. Car commercials. Classy ads. A select few opportunities screened by my agent that pay well and don't force me to play music.

Clooney and Nespresso have nothing on me.

I grab Annie's wrist and tug her toward the second bedroom, where I throw open the doors. It's got a king bed and a big closet.

"There's no ensuite." Her voice is flat.

"Adversity builds character."

Okay, maybe she's a little right. I have a lot of preppy shirts.

I stick sweaters and a few T-shirts on the shelf at the top of the closet. Most of what I used to wear is long since packed up in boxes.

The bathroom already holds the shampoo and shaving cream I like—at least some things never change, and Rodney has those on file.

I'm putting the suitcases under the bed when house phone rings. "Hello?"

"Mr. Jamieson, you have a visitor. I understand she used to tour with you."

Haley? It can't be.

"Mr. Jamieson?"

I hesitate. Annie's gone down to swim, her favorite activity that we share now. "Send her up."

I glance at the door, remembering when I'd been in the Ritz in Dallas and answered the knock to find Haley standing there looking indecisive and beautiful as fuck.

More than once since we parted, I've had a weak moment and thought of her.

Seeing her on the phone last week...

The red color on her lips it had me focusing on her mouth.

The things I did to that mouth.

The things I never got a chance to.

When Haley told me she'd move in with me two years ago, it was the best thing I'd felt since getting off tour. Maybe I'd been living in a dream, expecting everything would be simple once I stopped playing three cities a week. But it wasn't.

She was the bright spot in all of it.

Then she sided with Cross, with Wicked, and the floor fell out from under my world.

Shannon Cross screwed me from beyond

the grave, a final act that would have had him laughing in delight if he'd known.

I would've fought him for her. I would've fought anyone, anything, for her.

But there was nothing to fight, because she made the choice freely. She walked away first.

The knock on the door has me taking a steadying breath before I swing it wide to reveal the last person I expected.

A tall woman wearing a denim jacket and designer jeans with aviators perched on her fire-red hair is parked in the doorway holding a bottle of bourbon.

"So the rumors are true." She flashes her teeth. "Shannon Cross's prodigal son has returned."

"Damn," I drawl, resting an elbow on the frame. "A real live rock star at my door. How'd you find me?"

"We have the same manager, remember?"

The tension in my chest eases a few degrees as she wraps her arms around me. There are a handful of people I'll take a hug from. After touring nearly a year together, Lita's one of them.

I take the bottle of bourbon, and she

follows me inside. I pour two glasses before we sit on the low couch.

"Heard your last album went gold in two weeks," I say, passing her a glass. "I'm sure you got my card."

"Hmm. Must've got lost in the mail."

She looks good; Like she's gotten her share of the limelight and it suits her.

"You're selling out," I state.

Lita smirks into her glass. "Wicked has been good to me."

"I meant arenas."

"No, you didn't." She takes a sip. "What do you call what you've been doing, hmm? Giving the camera sexy eyes as you fake drive a fake car down a fake road in front of a green screen?"

"I call it keeping the bills paid."

"Bullshit. There are a lot of ways to keep the bills paid with that beautiful voice. You didn't run from music. You ran from Wicked." Her words have my spine stiffening even before she goes on. "You been back since the funeral?"

"Nope."

Haley and I haven't spoken either.

Sure, she texted me a couple of times the

first winter and left a voicemail asking me to call her back.

I couldn't deal with it. The wound was too fresh.

"She's not a kid anymore," Lita says softly.

It's as if she can read my mind. I hope it's because we've spent so much time together, not because I'm getting transparent in my advanced age.

"She never was, and that's the problem," I reply. "The first time she set foot on tour, she was her father's daughter. She wanted an empire. She got one."

"Come on. You might've been hiding out in Dallas, but you're not living under a rock. You know she sold most of her share of the company over a year ago."

I grind my teeth. "Makes you wonder why she went to the trouble of taking it over to begin with." I don't care what Haley's reasons were, but Lita's tone has something occurring to me. "Are you here for me or for Haley?"

Saying her name sends prickles through my body.

"She's had my back. You know Derek and the other guys can be every bit as fickle as

Cross. She's not like them. Or like him. Haley cares about the work, Jax. But more than that, she cares about the people." Lita glances around the room as though she's debating what to say. "When are you starting?"

"Meeting Monday."

"Good luck."

I toss back the rest of the bourbon, set the glass on the table with a clink. "You can tell her that."

Lita's laugh is light, tinkling. "Damn, I wish I could see that meeting. You're going to kill each other. Or—"

"I'm not here for her."

"Never said you were." She rises. "Thanks for the drink."

"You brought it."

"I did, didn't I?" With a grin, she slips out the door.

I can't resist calling after her. "Baseball season's right around the corner. Hope you had time to do your homework in between headlining."

She flips me off as she saunters away.

What Lita says doesn't change things one

bit. Haley and I aren't friends. We aren't lovers. The only thing we are is at war.

Haley Cross may have lasted two years at Wicked...

But she won't last an hour with me.

4

HALEY

One of my requirements when I gave up control of the company was that I kept my father's office. There have been changes since then, but some things—the fur rug in the conversation set, the big cherry desk, the Ireland picture on the wall—haven't moved. Changing the pieces that seemed most like him felt wrong.

"Haley."

Derek's voice has me looking up from my desk Monday morning. Derek's been around the block, and while he's not bold, he understands this place. He knew my father better than I did, having worked at his side for nearly ten years.

He steps inside, pulling the door half-closed behind him. Where Shannon Cross was always dressed for the red carpet, Derek favors slacks and sweaters.

"Jax Jamieson's coming in today."

"And you're afraid." My mouth twitches at the corner. After two years, I feel as though I can tease him a little. He has kids of his own and a sense of humor.

"Cross used to deal with Jax personally. I figured that might run in the family." He arches an eyebrow. "Given our unique deal, we agreed that you can call the shots on production, but I need to keep Todd involved since that's his department. " He glances at the clock. "See you in fifteen."

As he disappears, I let out the breath I was holding. Sometimes I forget so few people know Jax and I go back.

Wicked's rule about staff and artists not mixing hasn't changed since Cross's tenure. Not that anyone could fire me—I'm still part owner, and I don't take a salary—but Derek wouldn't be over the moon to learn about my history with Jax.

It's moot, because Jax and I are nothing, I remind myself.

I go over my plan before I collect Serena. "You coming?"

She looks up from her desk, a gleam in her blue eyes. "Let's see. The first and only guy who's ever got you hot and bothered is back and you're going to stick it to him. Plus," she amends with an eye roll, "I think I'm doing the release plan for the album, so yeah. Be there in two."

I make my way to the conference room.

Jax will be late. Although he had a near-photographic memory for the business side of the gig, he also knew that everyone here catered to him.

I expect him to put us off as long as possible. So I set down my things before taking a minute to look out the window, using the reflection to touch up my lipstick.

For the past five days, I've been wondering if this was even going to happen. I kept expecting to hear that Jax had called to tell us to go to hell. *It wouldn't be entirely unfair*. But the fact that he's in town does more than make my heart race.

It gives me hope.

"If I'd known it'd be the two of us, I would've brought drinks."

The low, familiar voice drags down my spine like a caress.

I cap the lipstick and turn, careful not to wobble on my heels. They're not what Serena would call "fuck me" shoes. No. These are "eat me" shoes—almost as high and pointier at the toe.

Jax fills the doorway. His shoulders are broader than I remember. His face is tan for April, and his jaw still a square angle. His hair is shorter at the sides, but still long enough on top to bend toward his forehead. He's too many steps away for me to stare at his mouth.

Small mercies.

Jax looks good. Better than good. In a collared shirt, and... Jesus, are those chinos?

"Wasn't sure I'd see the day," I tell him, my voice surprisingly level.

"When I walked back in here? Me either."

"I meant that you'd wear a belt without studs in it."

Jax rounds the table, his amber gaze sending shivers down my spine. Never once does he break my gaze as he spans the distance between us.

He stops inches away, his attention skimming down my dress, lingering on my legs. Then it drags back up.

Jax Jamieson is still walking sex. I can't tell if he's thinking about me or music or what he had for breakfast, but his firm lips and bedroom eyes threaten to destroy every piece of armor I've put on.

He hasn't aged, either. His face is strong and unlined, his nose straight, but as he leans, there's a tiny bit of gray in his sideburns.

It shouldn't be hot.

It's totally hot.

"Nice lipstick," he says, and I have to fight the urge to press my lips together.

I've watched him in the media and can't remember a mention of him with someone. But then, Jax has always been good at keeping his private life private.

His mouth skims my cheek as he leans in to whisper, "If you wanted to fuck me, Hales, all you had to do was ask."

My swallow fills the room.

"Am I interrupting?" Serena chirps from the door.

My eyes flutter shut for an instant, grateful for the reprieve.

Jax turns. "Skunk girl."

Serena drops her folders and phone next to mine on the table. "Pretty boy."

I take a seat next to Serena.

Jax drops into the chair facing our side of the table, looking around at the empty seats. "Let's get this over with." A knock sounds at the door, and Jax's face clouds with suspicion. "What's going on?"

Derek strides in with Todd. They're followed by a guy with long red hair, a blond, and one with dark hair, twirling drum sticks.

Jax stares at them as though he's seeing a parade of ghosts.

"Didn't I tell you, Jax?" My voice is light. "We got the band back together."

The look he shoots me is a mix of disbelief and incredulity, and it almost gets me back on even ground.

They say hello, exchanging bro hugs, except for Jax and Mace, who hug properly.

Mace murmurs something I can't hear, and Jax replies. They drop into seats next to him.

Derek starts. "Thank you for coming."

"You didn't give me much choice."

"Music's changing, Jax," Todd, Wicked's head of production leans in. "We don't want to let more time go on before finishing the contract we agreed to. Which is why we're cutting an LP."

Normally I don't give Todd a second look. He's narrow-minded and chauvinistic, but I can't help staring at him.

Jax beats me to it. "Full-length? Since when. I heard this would be an EP."

"It is." I shoot Todd a look, because we talked about this already.

The chance of going platinum—what I'd promised Derek—is higher with a full-length album. But I don't think I can keep Jax here long enough to get that out of him. It could take months. Years.

"We need to remind people who you are," Todd goes on. "Put you back on the map. That takes more than four tracks."

I wait for Jax to tear holes in the other man, but he shows a control that's new. "Right now we have zero," he offers.

"We have one," I interrupt.

"One track isn't an album."

"Then I suggest we get to work," Todd says smoothly.

I grit my teeth. "Derek?"

"An LP will make more of an impact," he says without looking at me.

Disbelief and betrayal compete in the back of my mind as Todd spreads his hands.

"So it's settled. Welcome back, Jax."

Todd grabs his files and stalks out, followed by Derek.

I shut my eyes. The sound of slow clapping has me opening them again.

Serena is already chatting up Kyle on the other side of the room. Mace and Brick are talking too.

I want to bury my head somewhere, but I force myself to meet Jax's cold gaze.

"This place has gotten real entertaining. You guys plan this good cop, bad cop shit?"

"It's a misunderstanding," I say as I round the table to Jax.

"Tell me something." The voice that has whispered all manner of sweet and dirty things in my ear cools more. "Who's producing this ten-track marvel? Todd? Because if that prick's in my studio—"

"The production team will be more than satisfactory. You have my word on that." No matter what's happened between me and Jax, he's an artist. I'd never ask him to do work I thought would compromise that.

His mouth turns up in a smirk. He's never been the tallest guy in a room, but he has the most presence. Some he built from being on stage, but some was always him.

I step closer, carried by bravado that's unfounded when I realize I can smell his masculine scent. I fight the shiver that works through me. "I get it, Jax. You don't want to be here. But to get this album done, we need a track list. If there's anything Wicked can do to help, let me know."

I meant it as a platitude, but Jax tilts his head. "How about some inspiration?"

His gaze drops to my mouth and I suck in a shaky breath. He's all physicality, all masculinity, and even though he's being an asshole I can't pretend to be unaffected.

"Those red lips could do a lot to inspire me, babysitter," he murmurs.

My stomach clenches.

In revulsion, because it can't be anything else.

I know he's screwing with me, because now I'm thinking of his cock. We did a lot of things together, but we didn't get to *that*.

In this moment, I feel every day of the more than two years we've been apart, because each one of them contributes to the strength I need when I respond.

"Derek's assistant will be in touch to book studio time," I say coolly. "I trust Annie was able to get into school. I took the liberty of having her books arranged. And I pulled some strings to ensure her teachers understand her situation and that they'll look out for her."

His startled expression gives me the tiniest hit of satisfaction before I walk out the door.

5

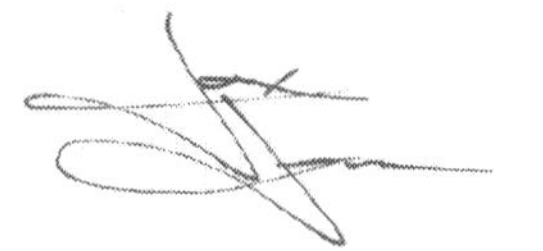

"You coming or what?"

I turn back to Mace. "Huh?"

"We're going down to Monk's for lunch and to talk about the album."

I tug on the collar of my shirt. He smirks but says nothing as we start down the hall.

Haley's talking with the woman who used to be Cross's assistant and Derek. She glances at us for the briefest moment, emotionless, before turning back.

"What'd you say to her?" Mace asks under his breath.

"Nothing worth repeating."

Hell, it wasn't worth saying the first time.

I should know better, but something came

over me. I went into that meeting prepared to play it cool. To get the upper hand and keep it. But since I walked in to find her, back turned, putting that lipstick on in her reflection from the window...

That dress doing mind-numbing voodoo with my brain...

The damn shoes making her legs even longer?

The plan degraded faster than my kid's good mood when she realizes we're out of Snickers ice cream.

Haley's always been pretty. Not the flashy kind that would break your neck from a distance. The kind you had to get up close to notice.

She didn't care about turning heads. She was always so absorbed in whatever problem she was working on—sometimes that problem was me—that it would be easy to pass her by.

But now, it's impossible to overlook her. She's got this confidence you can see in her straight back. The way her eyes survey a room. The sound of her voice.

She looks exactly the same and completely

different. But my thoughts aren't only about how different she looks.

I'm wondering if her new haircut—razor sharp with the edges grazing her collarbone—leaves enough length to wrap around my hand.

I shake off the haze of lust, because that's getting me nowhere fast, and we take the elevator down to the parking lot.

A Toyota Highlander sits in the lot, and Kyle rounds to the driver's door.

"What?" I drawl. "You got two golden retrievers and a house in the suburbs too?"

"Jump on in, boys," Kyle offers.

I shift into the back seat with Mace, and Brick slides in the front.

"How long have you assholes been planning this little reunion?" I ask.

"Not our plan. We just went along with it."

We drive downtown, and the atmosphere in the car is giddy. Monk's is an old favorite with mussels—a clincher for Mace—and the best beer selection in town. It's dark and wood and doesn't try to be anything it's not.

We claim a table, and Brick and Kyle go up to the bar to order.

Mace's phone beeps.

“That your girlfriend?” I ask.

“Notification from class. I’m taking art history online.” I stifle the laugh, but he doesn’t smile. “I’m serious. It’s interesting, and I like learning between gigs.”

I consider that. “You haven’t been around in a while.”

“You haven’t been free in a while.” He stares at me. “I know you have a kid. And I know that getting her was a rough year. But you’re doing douchey promo shit and not playing any music.” Mace folds his arms. “Annie still use my LEGO?”

“She’s thirteen.”

Mace cocks his head. “What’re you saying?”

Brick and Kyle return, setting four frothing beers on the table.

“So this album,” Kyle says, grunting as he drops into his seat. “What’ve we got?”

“You seriously want to do this.” I look around the three faces.

“Well, yeah,” Mace replies. “We’re on contract, but more than that, we’ve got a studio and rehearsal time. Wicked’s underwriting the album. One last push.”

“I don’t get why they’re doing it,” Brick says.

"There's no money in albums. And the contract wasn't for a tour."

"Could just be they need a front-runner," Mace pipes in. "Someone they can hook up-and-comers' names to."

"Or they have some other cash cows. Lifestyle advertising. Product placement. Music's just a way to get in the door," Kyle adds.

"Kyle's got a blog," Brick notes. "And I've been doing voice work for Titan Games," he says with pride.

Mace snickers. "They pay you in games?"

"I get real money, asshole."

I'm still wrestling with the reason we're here.

I don't know what happened in that meeting between Haley and the production guy, but something told me she hadn't planned it.

Still, the guys are genuinely enthusiastic about this, and I have to give Haley props. Using my band against me was a smart fucking move.

Looks like she got more from Cross than his company after all.

"So what've we got, Mozart?" Mace prods. "You know. For the rest of the album."

I drop back in my seat, tipping the beer to my lips. The woodsy taste of hops finds its way down my throat. "Haven't written anything."

"Haley says there's a song we can start with." Kyle shifts forward.

I raise my brows. "Really? What else does Haley say?"

Brick narrows his gaze, and Kyle smirks. Mace licks his lips as a plate of mussels is delivered and he descends on them. Three burgers come, and I reach for ketchup to douse my fries.

God damn, french fries are good. I'm going to be swimming an extra twenty laps to make up for it, but it's this or take it out on the band.

"So you and Haley," Kyle goes on. "Now that you're back, are you picking up where you left off? You know, necking like Romeo and fucking Juliet?"

"It's not going to happen," Brick notes.

Kyle frowns. "Why not?"

Shit, they could have this whole conversation without me.

"The other man." That has me straightening. "I think his name's Carter."

I nearly choke on a fry and wash it back with beer. The stein thuds on the table. "Carter?"

He shrugs. "I heard from Neen. I don't know the guy."

The bitter taste in my mouth isn't from the beer.

The dude she was on a date with was Carter. The pretty boy computer genius who screwed her over two years ago—who used her and tossed her aside.

Perfect.

Just because we're not friends anymore doesn't mean I want her with that asshole.

If I'm going to stick around this place for more than a few days, I need to know what the hell is going on.

"You're around a lot," I say to Brick. "At Wicked."

"Yeah. I'm not much for the politics, but after Cross?" He shrugs. "Derek was always good with numbers but rumor is he doesn't have the old man's baser instincts."

Which raises another question that's been

lurking in the back of my mind. "Why'd she sell?"

Brick exchanges a look with Mace. "I don't know, man."

"Find out." I force down a few bites of my hamburger, but it's wasted effort. I'm not hungry anymore. I'm torn between wanting to demonize Haley and morbid curiosity.

It doesn't matter what happened since we were together. She went her way and you went yours.

I grab my beer and shove her from my mind.

Annie's new school gets out before the one in Dallas.

Unfortunately, I don't realize it until too late.

On my way back to the hotel, I try her phone. No answer.

Inside our suite, I call her name.

I head down the elevator, and fear settles in my gut as I swoop out the doors to the main floor. "Rodney. You seen my kid?"

He nods toward the security guy, who

points at the screen. I round to take a look. She's in the pool, swimming laps. I heave a sigh of relief.

"She arrived home less than an hour ago," Rodney says.

"How'd she seem?"

"Like someone who'd finished her first day of school. Overwhelmed." He hesitates. "The pool's been closed for deck renovations, but I suggested she might like to try it."

His kindness gets to me. "You have teenagers, Rodney?"

"Not anymore."

"They survived, then."

"They did." He smiles. "The groceries you ordered have been delivered."

I thank him before making my way upstairs.

On impulse, I change out of the button-down, strip off my socks and tug on a T-shirt.

I want a shower, but I don't want to miss Annie coming back, so I cook.

It's another thing I never used to do. But in the past few years, I've gotten into it.

Though we have a chef back home who prepares most of our meals on the weekend,

I've learned to make some staples, including all of Annie's favorites.

When the door clicks open, I glance up to find her slinking in.

Her hair's soaking wet from the pool, and somewhere along the line she changed out of her bathing suit and into shorts and a sweat-shirt. My kid's always hot and cold at the same time.

"Hi, squirt. How was your first day?"

She looks taken aback. "Bolognese?"

"With"—I check the package—"soy curds."

My girl's a sucker for Italian, and it's easier than apologizing for dragging her across state lines with five days' notice. Something I hadn't thought about until Haley's comments.

I've never had to enrol my kid in school. I don't know if it's easy or hard. I know there's a shit-ton of email and paperwork to transfer over, because after the custody battle finished, my manager and lawyer handled it all when I had my hands full with Annie.

"Plus Caesar salad." It's my trump card, and her expression says she knows it too. "You need a shower?"

She shakes her head, sending her wet hair bouncing. "I did it down there."

With a moment's hesitation, she drops her swim bag and school bag by the door and approaches the kitchen. She pulls out cutlery and sets it on the coffee table in front of the TV.

"You have homework tonight?"

"There's a lot of reading. History and social studies mostly. I'm going to be behind."

Normally I'd tell her to get on it first thing. I didn't do enough homework as a kid, and I regret it.

"Tell you what. Why don't we hang out for a bit first?"

Her eyes brighten with interest. "Really?"

I grate parmesan on top of our dinner and carry the plates over to the coffee table. "Yeah. They can't expect you to be caught up on day one. We'll watch Netflix and chill."

She wrinkles her nose. "Don't ever say that again."

6

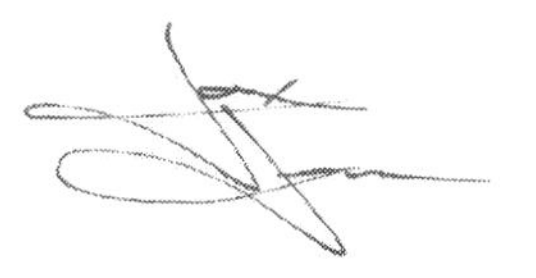

Being back in rehearsal is familiar and awkward at once. Like driving your favorite car with the seat in the wrong position.

We move around one another like ghosts, our gazes connecting and passing unspoken signals as we tune the track over and over.

"This doesn't suck," Mace declares Thursday as we finish running through the song I gave to Haley years ago. "I think it's there."

I lift the guitar off my neck and set it down before reaching for the full bottle of water next to the two I've emptied since lunch. "Let's do the bridge again."

"Seriously? We've been running this all week. I gotta meet Neen," Brick complains.

"I still can't believe you're tapping Nina," Kyle says.

"I can't believe it took so damned long," Mace weighs in.

"Ours is a forbidden love." Brick's grin is undercut by the wistful edge in his voice. "But seriously. Now that she's still running tours and I'm off 'em, it's all good."

I only half hear my friend's comments.

Part of me still can't believe Haley distributed the song to the band as an enticement to get them to come back. I always knew she had balls. But this is another level.

I hate it.

And admire it.

Three days here has me falling into a routine. Every morning, I wait until Annie goes to school before I head to the studio.

Every afternoon, I go back to the hotel, swim a punishing number of laps, then return to my suite and stare at the song I started as if I expect it to spontaneously multiply.

Because even though I told the guys I'm not making an album, they want to try. And though I haven't committed to anything, I find myself asking whether I even can.

More than once, I've caught myself thinking of Haley. Not what she's doing on the phone when I pass her in the hall, our gazes meeting for the briefest second. Or what she and Serena are laughing about in the kitchen when I go with Mace on a caffeine run.

I think of her with Carter.

What they do together.

Whether he knows what she likes.

When I'm not rehearsing, I talk some info out of the staff. She doesn't take a salary from Wicked, though she spends as much time here as she does at home. She lives in the old man's big Victorian house. She never finished her degree.

The last one bugs me.

A noise at the door has us looking up.

And dammit, it's the girl—woman, actually—I can't kick out of my head.

She's wearing them again.

Heels.

I miss the Converse, and it has zero to do with nostalgia.

These shoes are the same color as her legs

and make them look as if they go on forever. It's not that they're porn star heels either. They're only a couple of inches. But they're fucking fascinating because I've never seen her in them.

Instead of a skirt, she's wearing jeans. But ones that hug her hips, her legs. Her sleeveless top is black and dips in the front—fluttering fabric that skims her breasts and her waist. That has me remembering what it's like to touch each of those curves in turn, and the sounds I can coax from her when I do.

Her hair's raked back from her face and braided over one shoulder. Not in the way parents braid kids' hair. This has pieces falling out around her face, the ends spiky, as though she's already been doing something that messed with it.

No red lipstick. Her mouth is sheer and a little shiny.

I swallow the arousal.

"Howdy, Hales."

Since when does Kyle call her that? My glare goes unnoticed because mine aren't the only eyes on her.

"Guys," she says in that full voice that drags

down my spine like a promise. "How's rehearsal?"

Everyone turns to me, including her. Our gazes meet, and it's the longest we've looked at one another all week. Since we came face to face in the conference room.

"What've you got?" she asks, lifting her chin.

It's Mace who clears his throat. "Jax?"

I shift the guitar over my head once more, adjust the strap around my neck, and start our intro. We play the song again, and though I avoid her stare, I'm aware she's here.

That she's never heard the song.

That I wrote it for her.

I step up to the mic—not because I need it to carry my voice—out of habit, more than anything.

Playing the song is different than the times before, because she's here and even though I hate it, I can't help that part of me wants to know what she thinks.

We finish, and Haley's gone pale. Not enough for the guys to notice, but enough that I do. "It's sounding good." Her voice sticks in her throat, as if the words aren't quite right.

"Good. Think that's our first good, huh Jax?" Mace jokes. "Wait. No, it must be our second."

I shoot him a dirty look.

Because I sure as hell remember that first night she said those words to us in the elevator, but he shouldn't.

I meet Haley's gaze and the flicker in it tells me she does too.

"Right. I need the room in"—she checks her watch—"an hour. Can you pick this up tomorrow? Or somewhere else?"

"I'm outtie," Brick says, already packing up.

I slide my guitar into its case.

The other guys leave, saying goodbye to Haley on the way.

"What game are we playing, Jax?"

I straighten at the sound of her voice. "You're the one who hauled me back here like Domino Harvey. The bounty hunter," I go on at her blank stare.

If I'm trying to get a rise out of her, it doesn't work. Haley doesn't flinch, and that pisses me off more. "You're on contract for an album. All we want is for you to honor that," she says. "If you want to get this done and get back to Dallas, you might want to be more forthcoming. We need tracks."

I close the distance between us, raising a brow. "Forthcoming? Listen to you. You even sound like him."

And there it is. The flash that, for a moment, looks like hurt. But of course it isn't. I can't hurt her anymore and she can't hurt me.

My skin prickles when I realize it's just us in the room. The acoustics of the space are close to perfect, and every word, every breath, is fuller and rounder. More complete.

We're not complete. The thought comes at me from nowhere.

We're inches apart. I inhale a long breath, and I smell her. She's so different. I expected she'd smell different too. She doesn't.

She smells like pineapple, and that fucks with my head more than any words. Because it makes me think of how she used to be. How *we* used to be.

"Todd and I want to be ready to record in two weeks." Haley's oblivious to the internal battle that has my hands fisting.

"This the EP or the LP?"

She goes still. "EP."

"Sure about that? Last I checked, looked like some trouble in paradise."

Her lips part as if she suddenly has the urge to lick them. "Let me worry about Todd."

I smirk. "Whatever you say, boss. You want more tracks, you know the deal."

Haley's expression darkens. "I'm supposed to suck your cock in exchange for your cooperation."

Her flat tone has my shoulders knotting, even as the body part in question twitches.

Fuck, it sounds wrong. Desperate.

Nothing gives me the idea she'd wrap those perfect lips around my cock, even if I paid her a million dollars.

But damn if I don't want to see her admit it.

And that's what this is all about. I want to see the Haley I knew. The one with vulnerability. Not the new version who reminds me of a man I could never tolerate.

"I'm impressed you can say that with a straight face, Hales. You're all grown up. You kick the peanut allergy too? Burn all your Converse?"

We're inches apart, both breathing as though we've been running a race.

I've been in this room a hundred times. It's never felt like this. This tension, like a chord that won't resolve. It's her against me, and it's way more personal than our meeting in that conference room. This isn't about money, or fame, or attention.

These stakes are higher.

All it takes is the brush of her fingers over my belt to have blood flowing to my groin. "This is what you want, Jax? A cheap release to get the, ah…creative juices flowing?"

Her voice drops an octave and *shit*, I think she's teasing me right now.

I've crossed a line, but I can't back down. I manage a throaty chuckle. "If you think you've still got it."

Except *still* is the wrong word, because in the times we were together, we never did this.

Sure, I thought about it every second of the damned day. But I naively assumed we'd have a lifetime to figure this shit out. That I would have months, years, to explore her. To show her. To worship her.

The things we did were new to her, but what I never told her was they were new to me too. I've never been with someone I was head over heels for, before or since. Every touch of her lips, her fingers, every sound she made, every expression on her face, was a gift.

So how the hell did we get here?

There's no answer in her face or the silent room around us.

I'm about to tap out of this messed up game.

Until Haley does something that renders me speechless.

She drops to her knees.

She fucking *drops* to her *knees*.

My stomach drops with her as her fingers find my belt.

She slides it open and lifts hazel eyes, shining with challenge, to mine.

I can't speak, can't move, when Haley's fingers find the button of my jeans and work the zipper down, one agonizing inch at a time.

And it's hard because *I'm* hard.

I realize it the same second she does, and a little sound escapes her throat.

"You want me to stop?" I'd swear Haley's voice shakes at the end.

My answering shrug isn't the least bit

casual with my hands clenched into fists at my sides. "You're driving, babysitter."

Her fingers reach into my shorts and brush the underside of my cock, sending a current up my spine.

One smooth stroke that has my head dropping back.

The fluorescent lights overhead burn my eyes, but I won't close them. Anyone with a pass could walk into the rehearsal room but I drop my chin, forcing myself to watch what's happening because I know it'll never happen again.

Hell, I'm not sure it's happening now.

I can't think of all the reasons this is wrong. I can't think of anything except how Haley's tongue presses against her lower lip when she pulls my cock out with hands that feel like silk.

I swallow the groan.

Any second, I'll wake up—or she will.

I can't breathe. I watch her watch me, each of us daring the other to back out of this.

Her lips part, and the second of hesitation, the tiny V between her brows, has my gut clenching.

Then she closes her lips around the head of my dick.

"Fucking *hell...*"

Her mouth is hot and wet and the best place I've ever been.

She sucks at my tip, adding her moisture to mine before slicking her hand down the shaft, and it's a shot of adrenaline to a dead man.

Each stroke has me shuddering, and I know I won't last. It's all I can do to keep my knees from giving out.

Every time she sucks creates a heavy drag that tugs at my balls and down my spine. The twist of her hand at my base, the brush of her thumb just below her tongue.

I try not to turn into a complete animal, but my hips thrust against her face as my fingers find her hair—tugging, yanking it from the braid. "Harder, Hales." My voice is raw. "Yeah, like that."

I wonder what it's like for her. If she's thought of this too. Since I came back, or when we were together. I wonder if she loves feeling me hit the back of her throat, or whether it has her on the same brutal edge I'm riding.

Her gaze meets mine, and her eyes are dark with what she's doing to me.

Her fingers move lower, finding my balls. And *hell*, this woman knows my body. Even if we've never done this, she remembers everything I like when it comes to her touch on my skin.

I don't think I've ever been this turned on in my life.

Sweat clings to my back, and I'm reminded why rehearsing in a dress shirt is a dumbass idea. My foot cramps and I don't give a shit. I'll cut it off.

Just as long as she never.

Ever.

Stops.

The groan torn from my throat is obscene.

So is the sound of her sucking me off, all on the backdrop of that tropical scent that hangs in the air like a dirty dream I'm never going to stop having.

I'm close, and it's an actual miracle I lasted this long.

"Holy God, your mouth..."

But instead of speeding up, she slows down.

The pleasure's turning into agony.

Need claws through my body. Hot and desperate and demanding.

"Now…" I pant. "Now, now, fucking *NOW*."

I grip her hair, moving her head up and down on my cock.

It's too perfect to last, and there's no fighting the desire building in my groin, the tension in my arms, the shaking of my abs.

It's so wrong, but it's so fucking right.

If we were gladiators in an arena, I'd be lying on the ground bleeding out and begging her to finish me.

She doesn't.

I wait for the suck of her mouth, the answering explosion in my groin.

It never comes.

The heat of her mouth is gone, replaced by cool air.

I blink as Haley shifts back on her heels. Rises in one smooth motion, her shoes bringing us almost to equal height.

Every cell in my body roars in protest. My erection bobs between us, a silent and painful reminder that something went very wrong here.

Haley's darkened gaze is on my face as she tugs the elastic out of her hair, runs her fingers through the mussed strands, and pulls it back into a ponytail that's too tidy for what we just did.

"What the hell was that?" I rasp.

She wipes her mouth with the back of her hand, smearing a streak of lipstick. "Inspiration."

Her throaty voice has my balls aching as my heart hammers in my ears.

"You're joking."

Her gaze rakes over me, dragging down my body. Lingering without a hint of embarrassment on my rock-hard cock before lifting once more.

"You look inspired enough to me. I want those tracks by end of day tomorrow, Jax."

She's gone before I can zip my jeans.

7

HALEY

"Thanks for meeting, Haley."

"Thank you for being willing to come here at the last minute."

The accountant sitting opposite me in my dining room—my father's dining room actually—has a few years on me, and she's a numbers genius.

"Can I get you a coffee? I make a mean Americano," I say.

"No, thank you."

I tug mine closer, wrapping my fingers around it.

I told myself I didn't want to meet in public, but in reality, I couldn't stay at Wicked another minute. Not after what happened this afternoon.

"Now." The accountant pulls out the sheets of paper. "I will say it's unlikely your after-school program will become revenue-positive. Unless you take Derek's advice and use it for PR, in which case it might have a secondary effect on other sales and deals."

"But they could," I insist. "The problem is that we need a sustained marketing budget and a continued push behind any of these artists. It's not a charity. These kids are talented."

"The problem in today's industry is that albums can generate attention, but unless you're Riot Act, they can't recoup the cost of recording. It's all in tours and deals with brands. None of which come until you've built a name for an artist."

"It's a Catch-22."

"Exactly."

Her pencil traces the lines of numbers, and I follow.

I was hoping she'd be able to help me find a way to cut costs or ramp up revenues for the program.

No luck.

"Can I ask you something?" she says after she finishes.

"Of course."

"I helped you when you wanted to sell the majority of your shares in Wicked. I remember it was a difficult time and completely understand why you'd want to step away from things." Compassion transforms her face. "But I see how frustrated you are with how it's run. Why stay involved at all?"

For the first time all day, I feel the smile tug at my lips. "Listen to this."

I pull up an audio file on my phone and hit Play. I watch her face as the guitar riff starts. Four bars, then Tyler's voice over top.

She narrows her gaze. Not because she's critical, because she's listening. I can watch the wheels turn in her mind, and although I can't read her reaction to the lyrics or the melody, I see that she's having one.

And that's the beauty of it all.

At the end of the chorus, I stop the song.

"I've always wanted to do something that matters," I say. "The software I've built and licensed has made me money. But I'm more interested in the human side of music. The way it's created, how it affects people in ways other than opening their wallets. These kids are my chance to find the next voice that will change the world. They need time and nurturing and they'll do it, I know they will."

It's already dark when the accountant's Lexus backs out of the driveway.

On impulse I go upstairs to my room and change into leggings. I pull a hoodie off my shelf and wrap it around me. Then I go back outside and sit on the step, pulling the cuffs over my hands and sighing in the cool night air.

I've turned over a dozen explanations for why I made the decision to keep Wicked going. Guilt over not getting to know Cross when I had the chance. Revenge in the form of getting back at him for leaving—twice.

In the past two years, I've pieced together as much as I can about the man himself. From his brother and niece in California—though they rarely saw him. From his employees and coworkers. From his house and the things inside it. From his vinyl collection, which I shouldn't have been surprised to find was more impressive than mine.

I'd expected to create a single cohesive portrait of a man. Instead, I found two.

A ruthless executive who would do anything to succeed. And a man with a passion he refused to let die.

It's impossible to know what Cross set out to do with his after-school program, but I want to prepare kids with talent for careers in music by giving them the know-how to support themselves.

A familiar shape limps up the sidewalk, interrupting my ruminating.

"Serena?"

"Nice sweater." I don't respond as my friend bends double in her fitness gear. "I was out for a run and thought I'd stop by."

I'm grateful for the fiftieth time my friend lives ten blocks away as I shift off the step and let her into the house. "No Scrunchie?"

"He can't keep up. His legs are like two inches long." She stretches in my foyer. "You ever going to sell this house?"

"At the right time. When I'm ready for a change." The place is way too big for me, but it hasn't felt like the right moment yet. I've been busy with one thing or another since the day I inherited it.

I head to the kitchen. The floors creak behind me, evidence Serena's following.

"Ran into Kyle on his way out of Wicked," she calls after me. "He said you dropped by their studio. Funny thing is, I didn't see you after." Her voice is suspicious. "You want to tell me why you took off like your ass was on fire after dropping in to see our number one recording artist in the rehearsal room?"

I turn, bracing on the counter. "Because I blew our number one recording artist in the rehearsal room."

Her eyes go round. Once in a while, it's nice to be able to shock her instead of the other way around. "Holy shit. I'm surprised they didn't hear him on the third floor," she says.

I stare up at the ceiling. "I didn't let him finish."

The laugh that bubbles out of her is inappropriate and completely needed. "I love you, Haley. You should've asked him for a tour. A yacht. A diamond-encrusted skunk charm bracelet."

"That last one is for you."

"Yup." Her grin fades. "You okay?"

I nod tightly. "Yeah. I'm good."

Except that you yanked down your ex's zipper and went all amateur-sword-swallower on him.

I don't know what possessed me except that when he was staring at me—daring me—I wanted to show him I've grown up. That I can survive without him. That I'm not deferring to his age, his experience, anymore.

For his part, Jax hadn't behaved as he was supposed to either.

I sure as hell hadn't expected the intoxicating feel of him in my hands, my mouth. The groan of arousal in his throat. The "harder, Hales" that nearly destroyed me.

It killed me to stop.

In the end, I didn't do it to punish him. I did it to save myself.

I've done a lot of things in two years, changed in more ways than I can count, but seeing him come? Watching those amber eyes I used to love turn gold with satisfaction? Feeling him fall apart under my hands?

All of it would take me over an edge I'm so not prepared for.

I chew on one of the hoodie's laces. "It's not

fair. It's like he comes back and I'm *awake* again. I can't look at him without thinking twisted thoughts." Even now, I press my thighs together at the memory.

"Are you going to tell him what happened after he left?"

I swallow. "This isn't about that. I want to get the album made so I can get Derek off my back about the program. If we help these kids, they're going to be the future. Did you hear the track Tyler's working on? He's a great song-writer. And he has the most beautiful voice."

"Yes. And you have helped them. You've given them space to record. Some of them might become professional musicians. Others turned their lives around and credit this program."

"It's not enough. I want them to explode."

"You can't plan another Jax. Not for your-self, or Cross, or the world." I feel her stare on me, hard and compassionate at once. "But if you want to give these kids something that matters? You have."

I start wiping down the counters for some-thing to keep my hands busy. "I think about how Jax saved me. When my mom died. When

I didn't know where I was going or what my future held. The times I wasn't sure I had a future." I take a breath as I rinse out the sponge. "I don't want to save these kids. I want these kids to save the world. And I can't say that to Derek or any of the guys in suits that run Wicked. Because they have business degrees and look at numbers and market research all day. But that's not what this is about, not really, and I don't think that's what it was about for Cross either."

"How can you have two dead parents and still be this idealistic?" Serena groans, folding me in a hug that has me dropping the damp sponge and bristling until I force myself to relax. "Sorry, but you deserve this," she murmurs against my hair.

8

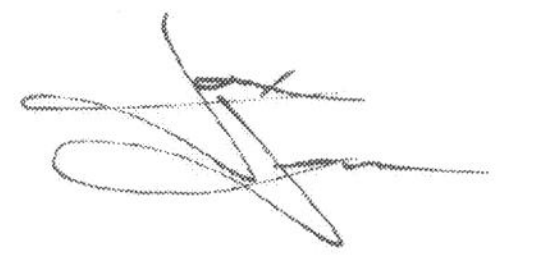

Now I'm truly fucked.

The dozen sheets of paper, laid out on the table with a care I usually reserve for instruments, tell a story I don't want to hear.

Each is the start of something. Some have chords marked on them, or guitar riffs that caught my attention long enough to be captured. A few phrases, sometimes a verse.

"Northing's good enough," I summarize.

Mace shifts forward, scanning the pages. "Try writing prompts?"

"I'm not resorting to Google."

Behind him, the hotel bar is quiet, but the occasional person trails in the front doors.

Enough to keep my busy mind distracted from the problem at hand.

I knew it on some level. I painted myself into this corner by coming back here.

No, it was before that.

It was two years ago when Haley sat across from me in my Bentley, looking at me like the sun shone out of my ass, and I gave her that song. Said she could keep it.

That moment of delusion was the root of all this fucked-up-ness because I gave her the one thing I wrote that didn't suck and now she thinks there's more like it.

"You need to send over two completed songs today because of... what?"

"Long story."

If I sound strung out, it's half about the songs and half about the phantom pain in my balls that's lingered since yesterday. The shitty sleep I got last night because I couldn't think of anything except those melted chocolate eyes.

Even though Haley didn't finish what she started, I can't go back on my word.

Yeah, when a girl half-blows you in exchange for songs, it's a regular moral dilemma.

Mace goes on. "I get that it's hard. The first

album was the best because you had nothing to prove. You were metaphorically bleeding on the proverbial floor."

I blink at him. "Art history, huh?"

He shrugs, shoving back his long hair and reminding me of one of Haley's philosophers. "You had nothing to lose. It was an escape. I know what that's like, to feel like you need music. That you can't live without it."

Guilt hits me. It's been a while since we've talked. "You don't feel like that anymore."

"No. Not to say it won't ever come back. Depression's a beast." Mace takes a swig from the mug in front of him. "But there are ways to cope. The times you want to shut out the world are when you need it the most."

When did Mace get more mature than me?

Because he is. He's more thoughtful and well-balanced, and I missed it.

All of it.

I wonder what else I missed, shutting myself away the last two years.

It's not like I stopped living. I renovated six rooms of my house. Built a shed the size of a barn, with the help of one of my favorite reality show home reno guys. I fought for my kid, booked a bunch of appearances, and got into what's probably the best shape of my life.

But when I turned my back on Wicked, I turned my back on music.

Mace gets up to use the bathroom, and I tug one of the sheets toward me. I need to turn this into a song. I couldn't do it on tour. Who's to say I can do it now?

My phone buzzes and I reach for it.

Brick: We rehearsing today?

Jax: Not until I finish writing

Brick: K

Brick: PS you were asking about what's going on at Wicked. I found something

Brick: Haley does some mixing but mostly she's
in charge of this program for teenagers

Jax: Send me a link

Brick: There is none. It's on the DL

I stare at the text a long time.

The reason she's still there is a single program? One they don't even publicize?

It gives me more questions than answers.

"Jax?" Annie pulls out her earbuds, straightening as she approaches on her way from the elevator, dressed for school with her hair pulled up in one of those high ponytails again.

She drops into the chair across from me. I can't put the papers away fast enough. She grabs one. "What are you doing?"

"Annie, come on."

I reach for it, but she holds it away. "'*No part of you can make me feel. No substitute for being real.*'" Her gaze meets mine. "You're writing a song," she accuses.

I didn't expect to feel embarrassed in front of a thirteen-year-old.

"It's not exactly the soundtrack of my life," she goes on.

It's fucking terrible is what it is.

"But I like that it's about what's real. Too many people don't talk about that anymore. Everything's fake. Who you are, who you know—"

"You're in my chair," a gruff voice insists.

Annie squeals, her eyes getting huger than the time she met Beyoncé. "Uncle Ryan!"

She drops the paper and hops out of the seat, throwing her arms around him.

Shit, I haven't gotten a reception like that since… well, before she found out my sperm gave her those eyes. For a moment, I'm actually jealous of my best friend.

"Hey, kid." She won't let go, and he practically pries her arms off at last.

Mace drops back into his seat and Annie takes the one between us. But her attention's solely on him.

"I haven't seen you in forever. Do you hate me?" she asks.

"Never." She shifts into the chair next to the one Mace sits in. "How's school?"

"That place you have to get to," I remind her, checking the time on my phone.

Her face falls. "It's hard being in the middle of the semester." Her gaze darts to me. "Can I have a friend over this weekend? If I don't, people will think I'm weird."

I turn it over in my head, but the idea's appealing. "Yeah. Sure."

Maybe it'll be good for her. She hasn't asked to have someone over in the weeks since we got here. Or a couple months before that, come to think of it.

"Uncle Ryan, you should come for dinner. Tomorrow?"

He glances toward me. "I have a night class until nine. And then you have that thing."

"The thing?" I stare blankly at him.

"Party for Jerry."

Right. The guy's retirement is being celebrated in a ballroom at a fancy hotel down the road. He's like the father I never had, and I wouldn't miss a chance to celebrate him.

"Sunday then." Annie beams, dropping a kiss on Mace's cheek before shouldering her backpack and dashing toward the door.

I grunt. "When did you become God?"

Mace chuckles, and I go back to the half-written songs.

"It's perfection, Mr. Jamieson. If I may say so."

The tailor inclines his head an inch, and I

glance back toward the mirror, straightening my lapels. It doesn't suck.

I have half a dozen suits at home appropriate for a red carpet event. But for tonight, I want more. It's Jerry's retirement, and the man deserves the best. So Rodney called his guy for me and arranged to have something flown in on short notice. Altered on even shorter notice.

On my way out of the store, the call comes in. I sling the bag of street clothes over my back, ignoring the stares I get on the street as I answer the phone.

"You on your way?" Brick asks.

"Yeah. Just have a stop to make. Forgot something."

"Mace isn't coming?"

"You know he hates these things."

I drive home from the tux alteration place and take the elevator up. I tap my fingers on the handrail.

After hours picking my guitar, a pencil stuck behind my ear as I scrawled changes over the paper, I have a grand total of nothing. The feeling of failure curls in my gut.

But I'm not going to leave Haley hanging.

The doors open, and I span the foyer in a few steps. "Annie, forgot to grab my..."

The floor tilts.

Because my kid is sitting on the couch.

With a boy.

At least I think he's a boy. He has blue hair.

There are two comfy armchairs, but he's next to her, laughing at something she said.

My hands tighten into fists. "What the hell is going on? Who are you?"

"Tyler, Mr—ah—Jamieson." His eyes widen, and he lifts his hands as if I'm about to do something illegal.

Maybe I am.

"Get the hell off my couch."

He rises, but his gaze goes to Annie.

"Jax." Her voice shakes. "Don't do this."

I ignore her, turning to the kid. "You're not talking to my daughter. You're leaving."

"Mr. Jamieson, you don't understand—"

"JAX!"

"I understand fine. Get out of my house."

With an apologetic look at Annie, he grabs his bag off the floor by the door and yanks on his shoes.

I turn back to my daughter as the door closes behind him.

"What was that?" she shouts. "You said I could have a friend over."

"I meant a girl."

"What does it matter?"

"Boys want things."

"And girls don't?" Annie's eyes flash.

"Jesus, this isn't happening." I hit a button on my phone. "I need a babysitter tonight. I know. I owe you one."

9

HALEY

"This isn't working," the small, panicked voice mutters from somewhere behind me.

I excuse myself from my conversation and move up behind him. "Need a hand?"

The kid turns, his eyes going round. "Wow. Miss Telfer, you look epic."

"Thanks, Mika. What's happening?"

He explains the issue, and I lean over the computer. The movement tugs at the cap sleeves on my dress, which was not built for typing.

I code for a few minutes then step back. "There."

The kid grins at me. “Thanks. And thank you for trusting me with this.”

The way he talks about handling sound for the party, it’s like it’s the biggest thing he’s ever done. It warms my heart.

“You’ll do a great job. Hey, is Tyler coming tonight?”

“He said something came up. Do you want me to call him? We were working on a demo this week. Mixing it with DRE.”

I get a kick out of it every time they use my program. “No need to call him. But I’d love to hear what you’re working on. Send it over. Or better yet, why don’t you come by next week? We can listen together.”

He beams.

I look past him at the room full of people. The stage, where the techs are finishing setup. Soon there will be speeches. Then the musical tributes.

The party’s at a fancy hotel, and Lita’s playing. The invitees may not include as many executives as my father’s funeral, but there are way more musicians, tour managers, and producers. Everyone who knows the industry knows Jerry, and tonight they’re here, wearing everything from black tie to jeans.

I settled on a gold dress that ends partway down my thighs and black heels Serena helped me pick out for the occasion. I curled my hair, bringing it up almost to my jaw line at the front. But really, the clothes don't matter. It's the collective spirit, the power, the love that matters.

I made sure Jax got an invitation, but as I look around, I don't see him. I hide the disappointment. Not because I wanted to spend time with him. Because he sent me the world's shortest email saying he has some tracks and will get them to me soon.

We're running short of time. Todd stopped in my office yesterday afternoon to ask what the hold-up is. I stalled him. I won't be able to stall him much longer, and the fate of the program that means everything to me hangs in the balance.

At least Todd's away this weekend. Golfing in South Carolina, I think. He's probably the only person in music who declined to change their plans to be here tonight.

When the evening program starts, Derek

does introductory remarks. When he calls me, I go up to the raised platform at the front of the room and take the mic.

"Gerald Timms"—I raise my brows and people laugh—"is a special person. I'm the least qualified to be talking about his contributions to music. But I couldn't pass up the chance.

"When I was on my first job with Wicked, he was the sound manager. He taught me everything I know. Which still isn't half of what he does. More than that, he taught me what's important in this industry."

My gaze finds Jerry at the front of the crowd. He's shining. Practically beaming.

I know he's struggled the past two years, but I've done everything I can to help him. Through medication the dementia is managed, if not solved. I like to think that keeping him engaged in music, his lifetime love, is helping to slow the disease.

"He's made a lot of friends in this room. He's had a profound impact on all of us. He'd never tell you this himself, but he matters. In every artist he's touched, every venue he's graced, every album he's charmed, and every intern he's inspired. To Jerry." I raise a glass, and they all toast.

After, I introduce Lita and hug her when she comes on stage.

I leave the stage and hug Jerry.

"Nice work, Miss Telfer," he murmurs.

A smile rises up from nowhere. Something he's always been able to conjure in me.

I wind toward the back of the room, offering hellos and thank yous as I go.

When I get to the back of the room where hors d'oerves are laid out on elegant silver trays, I choose a phyllo-wrapped mushroom and pop it into my mouth.

"I'm surprised you didn't ask me to play." The familiar voice at my back has me freezing.

I turn, half expecting to find Jax in a T-shirt and jeans.

He's not.

Jax Jamieson is dressed in a tux.

A goddamned tux.

And he's beautiful.

His striking jaw is the same strong angle as always. Those amber eyes are a little too light to be real. His hair is shorter than he used to keep it.

He looks like a prince.

That's the only reason I can come up with for why I lose the ability to chew and swallow.

Pieces of pastry and mushroom stick in my throat.

Now I'm coughing, the sound masked by Lita's music.

But Jax's attention's all on me. "You okay?"

I hold up a hand, shaking my head.

Jax looks past me to the table, his gaze landing on a tray of chocolate covered nuts. Moving faster than I've ever seen him move, he grabs a passing waiter, who nearly drops his tray. "Are there peanuts in there?" he snaps.

Oh, fuck.

"I don't—"

"Call 911," he thunders. "This is an emergency."

I shake my head, coughing, and grab Jax's arm.

"Hales, I'm going to get an ambulance. Hold onto her," he says.

The waiter closes in, uncertain, and I ward him off with my hands.

Jax curses. "Right. Strangers are bad. Don't hold onto her."

Finally I lunge for a drink off another passing tray and chug it down.

My throat clears and I gasp for breath. "Jax. It's okay. It just went down wrong. We always do peanut-free catering."

The panic recedes after a long moment and Jax relaxes. "You scared the shit out of me."

"Thought you'd just as soon have me dead."

I reach for a second drink off the tray and pass him one.

His brows draw together on his forehead. "Don't ever say that, Hales." He lifts the drink to his lips, sipping as he raises a brow. "Bulleit?"

My mouth twitches. "You know it."

When the waiter disappears, Jax shifts closer to my side, surveying the room.

"Thanks for saving me. And in a tux, no less," I say. Jax glances down at my dress. "Nothing? You're not going to tease me about the shoes? The dress?"

Jax tosses back the rest of his bourbon, setting the glass on a tray of a passing waiter. "I've made millions with words. Every time I see you, I can't think of a single one."

His careless admission slams into me, warms me like the liquor.

If he wants me to read into that, I'm doing it. Even though part of me expected him to come tonight—he's worked with Jerry as long as anyone—I could hardly have expected *this* Jax. Because it makes it harder to remember we're not friends. Or anything.

"I'm surprised you didn't bring someone tonight. Like Carter," he says, so smoothly I think I've misheard.

"Carter? Why?"

Jax lifts a shoulder under his fitted jacket, and it's totally not fair that he wears that and T-shirts equally well. "Heard you were dating."

"He's my business partner."

"That's all?" His gaze intensifies.

I feel my mouth twitch at the corner as an old memory comes back. "I kiss who I want, Jax Jamieson." His brows draw together. "But from here on in… Carter's just business." As I say the words I realize they're true.

Apparently satisfied, Jax nods toward the front of the room. "So he's finally willing to retire."

"He'd been planning to do it sooner. He

talked to my father about it and they agreed, but once Cross died, Jerry stayed to help with the transition. I ensured he was always compensated well."

"'Well' is a number guys in suits cooked up around a square table," Jax muses. "You don't pay a guy like Jerry well. He's a genius. Fucking Mozart. I can make them show up, but he's the one who makes them cry."

I hate when Jax goes all sentimental. Or his version of it—compliments doled out with the kind of certainty that preempts any objection. It reminds me how deep-down decent he is, in a way few people will ever truly appreciate.

"You love him," I murmur.

His gaze turns on me, surprised. "I'm not sure it's a good thing, being loved by me." I want to ask what he means, but before I can, he goes on. "The guy's going to have a hard time leaving this place. What I don't know is why you're still here. You sold the company. You can't move on?"

I hesitate. I hadn't wanted to involve him in this, but now that he's asking, it's hard to say no. "Cross started a program years ago. I took it, changed it. We help kids who don't have access to music get a chance to play. To record. To find their voice."

"Who's we?"

"Okay, me," I admit, taking another sip and shifting so some partygoers can pass us. The consequence is we're close, inches apart. "This one kid would blow your mind. His family situation sucks, but he's got incredible instincts for music. It's like all the shit he goes through pours out of him. I'd love for you to meet him. Tyler looks kind of crazy, has blue hair—"

"Tyler?" Jax's face darkens, and I wonder what I've said. "That little shit was on my couch this afternoon. With Annie."

My brows shoot up. "What were they doing?"

"Talking."

I wait a beat. "That's it?"

"Laughing," he amends pointedly. "Together," he says, as though I'm being deliberately obtuse.

"They go to the same school." I'd helped him get into the private school on a scholarship last year. Though most of the kids I work with are in public school, I convinced his mostly-absent parents this would be an opportunity for him. "I was hoping to introduce them, but it sounds like they already met."

Jax glares and I try to hide the smirk because damn, he's entertaining when he's protective.

"You're being a hardass," I inform him. "Trying to control things you can't control."

"I don't want her screwing up."

"Screwing up or growing up?"

Jax rubs a hand over the pressed line of his mouth.

"You know, part of growing up is being able to admit your mistakes," I murmur. "What happened in the rehearsal room... it was unprofessional. I'm sorry."

Jax moves closer. "I asked you to blow me in exchange for songs—admittedly not my finest moment—and you're apologizing to *me*?" He raises a brow.

"Yes." I feel the flush crawl up my cheeks under the intensity of his stare. "Come on, Jax. You know I wouldn't have done it if I didn't want to."

His mouth twitches. "In that case, apology accepted. You left me with the worst case of blue balls in history."

I can't resist laughing when a man says 'balls' in a five thousand dollar suit.

My nerve endings are tingling all over again, partly from his dry comment and partly from thinking about what went down between us.

"I got the sense you were more than enjoying yourself," I counter.

"I was. Until I wasn't." He shudders as if he's remembering the moment I pulled back. It would've been funny if it hadn't taken everything in me to do it.

He reaches into his pocket and holds out a flash drive. "A deal's a deal. Mace and I spent all day on the songs. But I'm not sure they're what you want."

"I can't wait to listen to them." I take the drive from him.

"They're not right, Hales."

His brows draw together under his hair in worry, not anger.

My chest constricts. Seeing him in this kind of self-doubt is agonizing. "Jax… I get that it's hard. Coming up with something new. But it's always been in you."

He jams his hands in his pants. "Oh yeah?

You going to share some eternal wisdom from some dead white guy?"

"I don't need it. I always had faith in you."

Jax's jaw works but he stays silent, as if he's weighing the words in his mind.

"I was surprised to hear from you after two years," he says finally.

"It wasn't two years. I tried to get in touch with you the winter after you went back to Dallas."

"You're right." Jax looks past me at the room of people, the laughter, the partying. "I should've called you back."

I take a drink, remembering the first text in January. The second in April. The bourbon blazes a soothing trail down my throat.

"I was fighting for my kid," he continues. "At least, that's how I rationalized it. But I was nursing my ego too. You walked away from me and it took me a long time to come to terms with that."

"You were the one who stopped us," I correct, going on before he can interrupt. "But you were right. We wouldn't have worked. I wanted to build something that was mine. You wanted to step away from it all. We were out of sync." My chest squeezes as I turn it over for the millionth time. The pain is nearly gone after two years, and what's left is just an echo. "But it's okay, Jax. We can spend our lifetimes regretting. Atoning. For the things we chose, the ones we didn't. That's not why we're here. Our job isn't to regret. Our job is to live."

"That's very mature for a woman with a Betty Boop clock." His amber gaze searches mine, serious and intense and full of an emotion I can't decipher. "What would you have said if I had called you back?"

I straighten, drawing in a breath and holding it. "You really want to know?"

"Yeah. I really do." His gaze is open and curious, and this Jax is the one I remember. The one I can't say no to.

"The first time was because I was pregnant. The second time was after I miscarried."

10

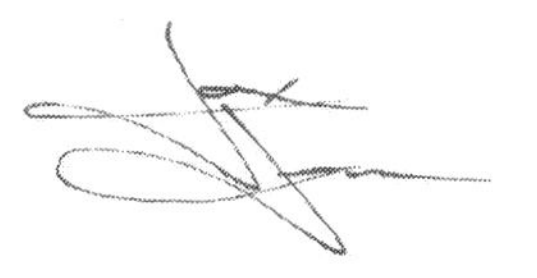

Music fills the ballroom. A third progression, my brain says. I hate that part of it goes there even as Haley murmurs an excuse, turns on her heel, and vanishes into the crowd.

Pregnant.

Miscarried.

Go after her. My body is heavy. My feet are lead, my stomach an anchor.

"What's with the monkey suit, son?" The man stepping between my target and me is the only one who could slow me down.

Jerry is a foot shorter than me, but it feels like I'm looking up to him.

Always has.

I force myself to focus on his lined face. "Heard some famous guy is retiring. You know who it is?"

He laughs.

"What're you going to do with all your time?"

"Garden." His knowing eyes search mine. "You'll be okay."

"I will if you will." But my gaze drifts back to Haley across the room, my fingers flexing. Her back is straight, her face focused on what she's hearing.

I wonder if he can read my mind. "She was a hell of a girl. Now she's a hell of a woman. She's had to take on a lot. For all his faults, Shannon wanted the best for her. He would've been bothered by how much she's been through. But proud of how she's handled it."

"How do you do it, Jerry?" My voice is low enough only he can hear.

"What's that?"

"Decide you haven't screwed everything up."

His milky gaze crinkles at the edges. "That knowledge is beyond us. All we can know is that we've done the best we can. Made some good music along the way."

I want to claw at my collar. To rip off my jacket and run outside and bellow. Because this is wrong. All of it. We shouldn't be in here, drinking expensive champagne. People shouldn't be smiling at me and prodding me for info about the new album.

I've fucked up. In a way you can't come back from.

I start toward the door but get interrupted by industry execs.

It's half an hour later when I spot her again. Surrounded by a group of suits.

I start toward her, intending to interrupt, but pull up halfway there.

She's smiling. I can't tell if it's forced or real but regardless, what am I going to say to her?

She's past it.

This is mine to live with, to wrestle with.

The car takes me home, and I ride up the elevator. I jerk the bowtie off, unbuttoning the top of my shirt.

When the door opens, I see Annie and Mace playing cards on the coffee table. Her smile falls away when she sees me, and she stalks into her bedroom, slamming the door.

"Thanks for the save," I tell him.

"No problem." He rises, brushing off his jeans as his gaze runs over my tux. "You okay?"

I strip off the jacket, hanging it on the back of a chair in the dining room. "Forgot how intense it is."

"I bet."

"You want to stick around for a drink?"

"Nah, I gotta go do some schoolwork. A paper to write on Caracci's *Hercules*."

After Mace leaves I go out onto the balcony, a crystal glass in one hand and Lita's bottle of bourbon in the other. I pour two fingers into the glass, inspecting it. It's good liquor. The kind I never had until I started on this twisted, beautiful journey.

I toss it back and pour another. The glass dangles from my fingers as I look out over the skyline, twinkling in the night.

"The first time was because I was pregnant. The second time was after I miscarried."

I feel it. The instinct to regret, to atone. The one I'd never noticed until she pointed it out.

"We can spend our lifetimes regretting what happened. Our job isn't to regret. Our job is to live."

Jerry's retired. Haley's spent two years alone. Annie hates me.

All I ever wanted was to protect the people in my life. Where does that leave me?

Alone.

I'm alone in the dark with the feelings I can't keep inside. Nothing matters. Not the money, not the recognition.

I drink the second glass, noticing every bit of flavor.

The empty crystal clinks on the glass table.

I go to my room and pick up my guitar.

Two moments fight in my memory for the worst moment in my life.

Neither was when my mom was arrested for dealing drugs and I learned she was going to jail, though it felt like that at the time.

No.

One was when I found out about Annie, that Grace and Cross had been hiding her from me.

The other was when I realized I couldn't provide for myself and my sister. I made her go to school, where she'd bum food from friends. We tried to put on a brave face. We used to joke that the sounds from our stomachs were monsters trying to get out. I spent the days in the library, which was open until midnight, where there were private rooms with computers. This one woman let me bring in my guitar.

One night, I went home to hear my sister crying in her sleep.

I swore I'd protect her and do anything it took to stop her from being in pain.

That reality is a million miles from this hotel. The expensive carpet under my thighs. The soft lighting overhead.

But the emotion connects me to it.

My fingers move over the strings, and it might as well be my first guitar that I got from a secondhand store and learned to tune and play myself.

I croon under my breath, nonsense mostly.

The door creaks at my back but I can't stop. It's spilling out of me as though I've sprung a leak.

"Jax?"

Annie's timid voice makes me stop singing. But my fingers continue, floating from one chord to another. I look up. She hovers in the doorway. Probably trying to make sense of her father sitting on the floor, back to the wall, playing his guts out.

She looks like me, like Grace. Her hair is redder, but her eyes are the same. They lighten to caramel when she's excited or upset.

I always thought Annie was like Haley. A little serious. Way too smart.

We could've had a child by now. Haley and me.

Would he or she have grown up like Annie? Would they look like me? Like Haley? Would they call me dad, like Annie won't?

Annie's gaze drops to my guitar. "I haven't heard you play in... ever."

Instead of defending it, I tell her the truth. "I haven't needed to."

She pads inside and shifts onto the corner of the bed.

"Tyler and a couple of other guys from school play at Wicked. Like you do." She hesitates. "I know you think it's weird that I don't hang out with girls. But the girls don't like me."

My jaw tightens. “What do you mean?”

She plays with the cover. “They say things. About you.” Annie looks up and misery fills her expression. “They talk a lot about famous people. Famous guys especially.”

I have to stop myself from shutting my eyes. Leaning my head back against the wall. “And that’s why you don’t make friends with them.”

She nods.

“Was it the same in Dallas?”

Another nod. “It didn’t used to be this bad. Just this year.”

The tentativeness in her voice makes me wonder how many thousands of thoughts go through her head every day that she never shares. How many experiences she never lets me in on.

I see her each day but it’s as if she’s a stranger.

My fingers switch, and I’m playing something else. There are no lyrics. It’s just chords, vibrations. The kind that take hold of your heart. That shine a lantern on the path ahead and tell you where to go.

Haley might disagree with me, but when you’re spilling your guts through a song, that’s not healing pain. It's opening it up, exposing it to the light. Diffusing it through a crystal so you can see it and share it and decide what it means.

I don't know the words that make pain go away. If I did, I could rule the world.

"Sometimes I think I hate you." Annie's small words are uttered quietly. "But even when I think that, I still want to know you."

Her earnest face has my heart squeezing. "Because I have three Grammys and got you that signed Timothée Chalamet picture?"

"No. Because you're a good cook. You bite your nails even though you try to hide it. You think watching documentaries counts as homework. You hum when you drive." She shifts closer, bracing her elbows on her knees to bring her face level with mine. "And because you care. Some of the other kids at school... they have all this money, but it's like their parents don't even care what they do. Sometimes I wish you cared less. Then I take it back. Because I don't. Not really."

My chest expands, stretching my ribs until it hurts. If there's a way you're supposed to handle this I have no fucking clue what it is.

So I stop trying.

I brush my thumb over her chin. "Good," I say finally.

I go back to playing, and she shifts forward to lie on her stomach, a smile painting the edge of her lips as her eyes drift closed. "That's pretty."

"It's nothing."

"It's still pretty."

My song finishes, my fingers stilling.

"Are you writing it down?" she asks as the final sound waves die.

"No."

She leaps off the bed and runs out the door. A moment later, she's back, dropping on the covers again. Annie sets her phone on the floor in front of me. "Play it again."

11

HALEY

"You out for lunch?" I ask Serena when I call her on Monday afternoon.

"Yeah. You want to join?"

She gives me directions, and I meet her at the fast-healthy place. A familiar black-and-white fluff ball is in her arms.

"We had to go to the vet this morning," she informs me when I sit down.

"He looks very healthy."

"I think he's depressed. He doesn't play like he used to."

I debate how much to say. "He is..." I lower my voice as if it makes a difference, "...old."

"No way. Skunks live two to three years in

the wild, but they can live up to ten in a loving home. It's proof!"

"Of what?"

She sighs. "That all you need is love." I can't help but laugh at her over-the-top gushing. "Although it also occurred to me that maybe he needs another kind of love. You know." Her gaze narrows. "Something more physical?"

Oh, God.

"I thought about putting an ad on Craigslist for someone with a female skunk who wants to—"

"Don't finish that sentence. Or that ad," I beg her.

Serena sighs, looking past me. "Fine. I've put in our order, but you need to go pick it up. They won't let Scrunchie in."

I reach over to stroke a finger over his soft head. "Sorry, handsome."

I go in and grab our food, then come back to the metal table and chairs outside.

Serena lifts her sandwich off the tray and I reach for my salad. "So Jerry's party was bomb," she says. "It's been written up on five blogs in the last forty-eight hours."

"I saw you with a guy. Scratch that. A *man*."

I think of the tall, dark and confident form I'd seen her laughing with at one point.

"Jacob Prince. He's got a jewelry company."

The name scratches at my brain as I stab a forkful of lettuce and cheese. "Prince Diamonds?"

"The one and only. He's a New Yorker, happened to be in town for the weekend. We went to boarding school together."

"Really?" I chew, studying her face.

"The man's got issues, but all the good ones do. The stories our crew had... Skunk sex has nothing on boarding school, believe me." She grins and I'm almost tempted to ask. "But speaking of men too handsome for their own good, I saw Jax in a tux." She fans herself. "Tell me you were unaffected by that."

I reach for my pop. "Dead women were affected by that."

Her laugh makes Scrunchie jump. "I think I heard your vagina cry a little." Serena breaks off a piece of her sandwich and slips it to the hopeful-looking fluffball in her lap. He takes it, watching me with beady eyes as he munches.

I spear some more of my lunch, chewing and swallowing before I speak again. "I told him. About the pregnancy and the miscarriage."

"Whoa. What did he say?"

"Nothing."

"Nothing?"

I lift a shoulder. "I dropped it on him and then ran. He got to do it last time. Figured it was my turn."

"So he didn't have the decency to feel like a giant lump of shit for not getting back to you? I was ready to drag his ass back here, you know I was."

Her loyalty warms me as I set the fork down in the bowl. "I know." And he would've come back.

But I still remember the words I'd said to him in the shower after Mace was in the hospital. The promise I'd asked him to make.

Don't regret me. Ever.

"I don't want him to say he's sorry, Serena. To do anything out of obligation. That's why I didn't go after him when I found out.

"He loves Annie, but I saw on his face when he told me about her that he never wanted another mistake. I never want to be his mistake." I take a deep breath to combat the way my gut twists.

She squeezes my hand and my smile fades.

"He did come through in one way. He gave me the songs."

"And do they sound like a platinum album?"

Disappointment wrings through me. "They're not what we need." She grimaces. "I saw what it took for Lita's album to hit gold. I know Jax can do more, his fans want more. But it has to be real. Todd's breathing down my neck. I really think he wants to watch me break."

"Clearly he doesn't know you. So what's the B plan?"

"That was the F plan." I blow out a breath. "Something told me if I got Jax back here, got his band and a studio, magic would happen. Maybe it's not that simple. Maybe I'm missing something."

"Maybe he doesn't have it anymore."

My spine stiffens as objection rises up in me. I shake my head, hard enough to send my hair hitting me in the face and have Scrunchie watching me with suspicion. "No. That's not it.

The month I spent on tour, even the fall after that, I had this idea that my program would explain how Jax Jamieson does what he does.

"It got close, helped make good songs better, but even it couldn't take bad songs and make them good. Or great songs and make them mind-blowing.

"Because I realized something. Jax's magic isn't the words he writes, or the chords he plays. It's that he feels like no one else does, that he can translate it into this catharsis for the rest of us. But right now, he doesn't want to feel. He's opted out. I don't know how to change that."

Her smile is sad. "I love that you won't make it his fault. No matter what, you won't believe he's less than a god. Even after everything."

I rub my hands over my face. "You think it's stupid."

"I think it's sweet."

My phone dings and there's a new text. "What...?"

Jax: Hales. Thought you might want to check this out

Jax: We recorded it on Annie's phone.

I hit Play on the track, and sound streams out. The quality isn't great, but what I hear is.

My heart thuds. "Are you getting this?"

Serena's eyes widen. "Holy shit."

"Yeah."

I type back as fast as I can.

Haley: I love it

A few moments later, he texts back.

Jax: For real?

Haley: It's going on the album. Got any more where that came from?

Dots appear. Then he sends a sound file.

"You ever look at a guy like you're looking

at that phone right now, you'd have a boyfriend by now."

I grin. "Shut up."

Haley: You wrote two songs last night?

The dots appear again.

Followed by the most beautiful words I've ever read.

Jax: I wrote four

Studios never sleep. Some of the most iconic tracks in rock, jazz, and country history were laid down at all hours of the day and night.

Still, the regular staff tend to stick to the daylight hours. It's the big artists and a handful of execs responsible for the lights after dark.

Wednesday night in my office, the door is mostly closed and it's late, but I'm listening to a track that has my entire body buzzing.

It's not one of our big artists. It's one that matters more.

"What do you think?" Tyler stares at me from across the desk. His blue eyes match his hair, and though I've witnessed it blue, green, and black, I struggle to remember if I've seen its natural color. One foot's tucked up on the chair in front of him, not because he's casual but because he's nervous.

"It's really good. You cut the reverb—"

"Yeah, I ran it through DRE and it came up with some suggestions. But I also scrapped some of the recos." He shows me, his fingers flying over my computer keyboard to adjust settings. His gaze is as jerky over the screen as his voice is smooth over the speakers.

I nod as I listen. "Yeah, okay."

"How'd you even come up with the idea for DRE? Did you always want to make music better?"

I can't help smiling, because I love how this kid's mind works. He's always curious, always wanting to know why and how. "Actually, I wanted a way to explain the music that changed my life. The part about making music better happened by accident."

I hit Play on the song again and listen to the changes he made.

Excitement bubbles through me.

And shit, this is why I do this.

Once I thought the words mattered more than the chords, the melody. I was wrong.

Nothing matters more than anything else. All of it matters, together.

Movement from the doorway has me looking up.

Any instinct to chastise falls away when I see whose face it is.

The faded blue T-shirt hugs Jax's chest and arms, skimming over his abs, none of which seem to have softened over the years.

The jeans hang low on his hips, and I force my attention to his face.

Since he sent me the songs yesterday, he's been rehearsing, and I've been busy working too.

His gaze lands on Tyler, whose hands stiffen on the chair arms. "Mr. Jamieson."

"Tyler."

They stare each other down.

Is this is how bullfights start? Because Tyler looks like he desperately needs something to distract the very big and very irritated form in the doorway from charging.

I clear my throat, looking pointedly toward Tyler when Jax acknowledges me.

Finally, Jax speaks. "Kid. About the other night. I might have got the wrong impression."

Tyler nods vigorously. "You did. Annie's my friend. She's really cool. She knows more about music than anyone."

"Really?" That comment seems to throw Jax for a loop.

"Uh-huh. I mean, it makes sense. She has killer taste. The playlists on her phone are all over the place and she knows the entire discography of bands I've never heard of."

"She does?"

"You should get going," I say to Tyler. "The bus stops running soon."

"I brought my bike."

I shoot him a look. "It's not safe to ride that at midnight."

His lopsided grin, as if I'm worrying too much, has my chest expanding. "I'm good."

But he slides out of the chair and gives Jax a bit of a berth as he leaves.

Jax drops into the chair next to the one Tyler vacated. "Parents don't care where he is?"

"No."

Jax's chin drops, because he knows what that's like. "Been a while since I was here." He inspects the armrests before his attention returns to me. "The view from this seat's improved."

I flush even before his gaze drifts down my body. He stiffens.

"Hales?" The look on his face slips from curiosity to wariness.

"Yeah."

"Is that my hoodie?"

I pulled it on over my dress earlier. It looks ridiculous, but people don't usually walk in on me at midnight. "It's cozy."

"I didn't think you'd keep it."

I shake my head in disbelief. "Are you kidding?" I lean in, lowering my voice. "It's signed by Jax Jamieson."

His perfect mouth curves, and my stomach turns over.

I forgot how addictive it is to have him look at me like that.

“Um. The songs you sent are amazing. How’s rehearsal?”

“That’s what I wanted to talk to you about. We’re nearly ready to record.”

“Great. Derek will get you on the schedule.”

"Who's producing?”

I suck in a breath. “I was thinking me. And Todd.”

“No.”

The hurt cuts me quick. “Jax, come on—”

“I don’t want that asshole on my album. Just you. And Jerry. Apparently a few days into retirement and he’s already restless.”

My heart skips, and for a moment, everything in the world is bright. “Todd’s not going to like that.”

“Do I look like I care?”

The grin threatens to split my face.

No matter what we’ve been through, how close or how far apart, he’s still the biggest rock star in the world. I’ll always be in awe of him.

Jax shifts forward, the shirt pulling over his biceps and dragging my gaze to the ink on his arm.

I wonder if he’s gotten any new tattoos.

I wonder if he’d let me look for myself.

"You were right," he says.

I blink. "About what?"

"Annie. She's into music. I didn't know how much."

"She can come play with other kids if she wants." The words bump into one another, and I'm pretty sure I'm blushing. It's a stupid reaction, considering the things he's done to me and said to me. "I'll email the schedule to you."

He rubs a hand over his jaw, the few days of scruff there.

I want to be that hand. Or that jaw.

He leans back in his chair. It's my office, but he looks like a king holding court.

Jax's gaze skims the surface of the desk and lands on the corner. "Need a break?"

"No," I say too fast.

His amber eyes sparkle. "It'll only take a minute, Hales."

"Oh, you think so?" The challenge on his face has me shutting the lid of my notebook computer and sliding it off to the side.

He flashes me a grin. One of those devastating smiles that shouldn't be legal.

He reaches for the chess board at the

corner of the desk, careful not to disturb the pieces.

Excitement tingles through me.

"Last game was a blowout," he says.

"That was a long time ago."

He grabs two pieces, one white and one black, and puts them behind his back. I nod to one side, and he reveals the black piece.

"Go," I say.

He does.

My attention snaps from him to the board in an instant.

We play like old times. With one important difference.

"You got good," he says after a few moves.

I smile, toying with the string on the hoodie. "I still play at least twice a week."

Jax shakes his head, admiring my play. "You make any mistakes anymore?"

"Some days it feels like all I do is make mistakes."

The words are out before I can think about them.

The look in his eyes isn't judgment or sympathy. It's understanding.

He reaches up to pull on his hair, rubbing a

frustrated hand over his neck and dragging my attention up from the board.

When he speaks again, his voice is low and urgent.

"Hales. I can't sleep knowing what you went through alone." I swallow, fighting the emotion that threatens to rise up. "Is that why you sold Wicked? Because you miscarried?"

I find a smile. "I sold it because I was pregnant. I have enough money. I wanted time, and space."

His face fills with anguish. "You must've thought I was such an asshole."

"No. I was upset when we broke up, I'm not going to lie. But I don't blame you, Jax. It must have been hard when I chose Wicked. I know you hated Cross."

Jax leans forward, closing the distance between us. Moody amber eyes hold mine in a grip that won't let go.

"Not as much as I loved you."

Words have the power to take your life, to shape it.

To put your heart back together when you'd swear it was broken forever.

I wonder if he can see every emotion on my

face. Maybe he can, because his gaze darkens on mine, his throat working.

We're inches apart. Too far and too close at once. I'm desperate to change it, I just don't know which way.

Jax nods toward the board without breaking my gaze. "Your move, Hales."

12

HALEY

Jax is watching me.

His full mouth is pursed. Those amber eyes are glowing under his dark lashes, under the hair that falls across his forehead as if it belongs there. Under the T-shirt his shoulders are tight, his arms flexed.

It's intoxicating, the weight of his attention. Having the most beautiful man in the world watch you as though he's hanging on your next word, your next breath...

He's waiting for me to choose.

Before I'm even sure what I'm choosing from, every option fades away until there's only one thing in the world I want to do.

My hands hit the desk, braced under me as I shift over the board and crush my lips to his.

I'm home even before Jax opens under me, his mouth hot and welcoming.

Taking everything I have and giving it right back.

God, yes.

It's not a thought; it's a feeling.

He's all hunger and need and deliberateness as he rounds the desk.

Then his hands are in my hair, his body slamming mine into the wall as he kisses me.

Wild.

Desperate.

I forgot what it was like to be swept up in his storm. To be afraid to succumb to the hypnotic spell he weaves with his hands, his voice, his body almost as much as I'm desperate to.

It's *everything*.

He's everything.

Jax yanks the sweatshirt over my head..

My dress is gone nearly as fast.

The heat of his lips on my neck drives me crazy. I squirm against him, and his teeth nip my sensitive skin. Punishing me or encouraging me, I don't even know.

His shirt is next. That part's my doing because I can't stand the thought of the fabric between us. I want to touch his skin. See if he's burning up like I am.

My greedy hands roam his bare chest, and I exhale on a shudder. His muscles jump under my touch as I trace them from memory, and how is it possible this isn't close enough?

I want more.

All of him.

His arms band around my waist. It's surprisingly PG, except for the sheer force of them. And the insistent hardness pressing between my legs. I reach for him, hauling his mouth back to mine so I can taste him again. The dark flavor of his mouth combined with both of our desire.

Jax pulls back an inch and I blink my eyes open, startled to find wetness stinging my cheeks.

"Did I hurt you?" he asks.

"Yes." I swallow. "Don't stop."

"Fuck." His forehead presses to mine, the first beads of sweat forming there.

Jax's hands find my thighs under my dress. His heart hammers against mine, but he's slow as he skims up and under the hem. Amber eyes burn into mine as my eyelids threaten to drift down.

"Don't," he murmurs. "Look at me."

I do.

I'm twenty-four years old. I've buried both my parents. Worked a rock tour. Been kicked out of school. Run a record label. The kind of ups and downs that give you whiplash.

I've vowed never to let myself be at anyone's mercy ever again.

Yet when it comes to this man, I couldn't care less about all of it.

"Tell me you missed me," he rasps against my throat.

"Yes."

His touch strokes higher, over the curve of my hip. He palms my ass, his finger playing with the back of my thong, and his breath hitches. I yank my dress up as he pulls my knee around his hip. The friction of his jeans burns my bare leg.

None of it matters when his fingers brush between my thighs.

I bite my lip to keep from crying out. I'm soaked. I can feel it from my panties, from the way his fingers slide. He moves the fabric aside and I hiccup a breath.

"Hales." My eyes squeeze shut because I could come just from the way he says my name. But Jax has other ideas. "Since that day in the studio, all I can think about is doing this."

His fingers sink inside me, and my moan fills the whole office, like he fills me.

We're sharing the same breath now but not kissing, not really. My hands dig into his biceps, holding him or me steady as he drives me insane with need.

His thumb joins the party, stroking up over my clit in rhythmic passes.

I wonder if that's what playing a guitar is like.

The only noises in the room are our panting breaths and the sounds of him touching, teasing, filling me where I'm so turned on.

He builds me higher with every stroke.

I'm hanging on by a thread. To him, to consciousness. Every stroke of his hand pulls on me, and my muscles are so tight I'm shaking with it.

"I can't wait," I murmur, my fingers digging into his arms. My head falls back against the wall, and his lips cover my jaw.

"We've waited enough." His satisfied murmur against the shell of my ear combined with his touch breaks me.

I go stiff against him, trembling with the impact. He holds me up as I gasp and pant my way through it.

I don't know how I survived without this. Without him.

When I come down, he's tugging at my dress. "I need to see you."

With wobbly limbs, I help him get it off. Or maybe I make it harder. Who the hell knows?

Jax gets the damn dress off and hitches me up on the desk. His jeans get shoved down by impatient hands, then his shorts too. My hand wraps around his cock, and Jax hisses out a breath.

He lowers me onto the desk. I can't get enough of him. The hard lines of his body are the same. The muscles of his arms, his pecs. The light trail of hair down his stomach.

I play with it, making him curse.

"It's a miracle I can even get it up after what you did to me last week," he groans.

Chess pieces dig into my back and side, but I grin anyway.

He pulls back, his expression tight with need and something else as he traces a finger down my breast, along my side.

My throat turns to desert before I hear the rip of foil against the backdrop of our panting breaths.

Anticipation grips me. He's standing over me, wanting me as much as I want him.

He's between my thighs. Brushing. Nudging.

Jax lifts off me far enough to look in my eyes.

Then he sinks into me.

All.

The.

Way.

I'm underwater. Drowning in sensation. Gasping for air.

I adjust to him as he watches. His face is a mirror of mine. Disbelief. Memory clashing with reality. Past and present.

It's like listening to him play a song. There's

the familiarity of every time before, competing with wanting to experience it for the first time.

Until the past falls away and all there is is *now*.

He shows me with his hands, his body. Shallow strokes flattening out to deeper ones. Jax's hands find mine, our fingers lacing as he presses my hands overhead. My knuckles bump the cool, lacquered wood of the desk.

All I can do is thrust my hips up to meet his. The futility of it is soothed by the fire in his eyes.

I feel as if he's keeping me there. As though he's afraid I'll leave and he's using every ounce of his intention, his body, to make sure I never do. With that thought, the need takes over and has me crashing into him again as I cry out.

He shakes on top of me as his sweat-slicked body crushes mine.

13

My body feels like I just swam a hundred laps.

Then ran a marathon.

The kicker is, the second I meet her gaze, I'm ready to go again.

"I always thought this was creepy," Haley murmurs, trailing her fingers through the thick fur rug on the floor.

I manage a half laugh. "Me too."

I take in her body—flushed, naked. I could stare at her all night.

Somehow she's even more beautiful than I remember. Every inch of skin begging for my hands, my mouth. She's like a forgotten language, and I want to learn her all over again.

I swallow the impulse.

"The custodian'll have a field day if they find a condom in my garbage," Haley says under her breath.

"I don't give a shit if people talk. But you do." I realize as I say it it's true.

Haley's expression clouds as she pushes a hand through her hair. "My relationship with Derek and the other executives is complicated now that I'm not a majority owner. Finding out about our history wouldn't help."

I roll onto my side to face her. "Then they won't find out we fucked each other's brains out in your dad's old office," I decide.

Her mouth tugs up at the corner as if she thinks I'm sweet or cute or some other totally inappropriate thing given the circumstances.

I clear my throat as I cast my gaze around the office. "Speaking of. That was unexpected."

"Yeah." She wraps her arms over her chest, which only drags my eyes down. "When you said that thing, about how you loved me... I guess I got caught up."

"Me too." I rub a hand over my jaw, and Haley's gaze follows the movement. Interest stirs in my groin again because attraction's never been our issue. "It's been eating me up inside how we left things, Hales. I keep thinking how much I fucked up our ending."

The green flecks in her eyes dance. "You didn't fuck it up. I made a choice, and you made one too. I'm not broken, Jax."

"I know. You were always strong. Even when I met you on tour."

Her mouth curves. "We had some good times."

Just like that, she has me remembering those times. The bowling alley. Making out on my bus. The night she sang on stage next to me. That first day, sitting in the back of my limo. Me tossing her a bottle of water out of my bus.

My heart squeezes.

"It's in the past."

"Mostly." My fingers strokes down her arm and she lets out a little sigh.

"Mostly."

A noise in the hall has us both freezing.

"Tell me Tyler's gone for sure."

She snorts. "He is."

"Good." I stare up at the ceiling, counting

the pot lights there. "Listen. I'm tired of regretting. What if we had another chance."

Her hesitation nearly kills me. "With each other?"

"At an ending." I turn toward her again, and those chocolate eyes deepen with the need to understand. Something I've always loved about her. "It's like a three-minute song. The first half's full of possibility because you're just getting started. The second half's building to the end. You know it's coming, but you don't have to dread it. You can enjoy the third chorus, the bridge, because it's all part of it."

"Okay," she says slowly.

"So maybe doing this album together is a second chance at a first ending."

"The second chance at a first ending," she repeats, and her hesitation nearly kills me. "I like that. Deal."

For two years, I've been sure the chapter of my life with music, with Wicked, was over.

Now I know that's not true.

I wrote four songs this week. With a little work, they'll be damned good.

More than that, I feel alive. Like I'm part of something again.

Whatever battle Todd wants to have, I'm all in.

Because this album is *me*. My truth, for the first time in a long time.

It's a different truth than before, because I've lived ten lives in the decade since I wrote that first album.

Not all pain or joy can be experienced by a teenager. When you're grown, it has more shades, more nuance. All of it's in those songs.

As far as I'm concerned, Haley and I have unfinished business too. Whatever time we're not working on the album, I'll use to prove to her our last ending wasn't the right one. I won't leave her that way.

What if don't want to leave her at all?

The disturbing thought lingers in the corner of my mind.

I'm heading over to the studio the next day when I get the call that the principal wants to see me about Annie.

I park outside of the expensive private

school and find my kid. She walks with me to thc office.

"You seriously don't know what she's going to say?" I ask.

Annie shakes her head, looking nervous. "No." Annie starts to wait in the hall, but I motion her in with me. Her brows rise. "You want me to come?"

"Yeah. You might as well hear what they're saying about you."

She swallows her surprise, sticking to my side.

"Mr. Jamieson."

The principal, a sixtyish woman who looks like a poster for Newport living, welcomes us in. We take our seats across a cherry desk which I now know from my construction projects would cost a lot of textbooks.

Desks. That's what the tuition money goes to in these places.

The woman clears her throat. "Anne has put some inappropriate material in her locker."

"What kind of inappropriate material?"

She shifts. "Photos. Of men." My back straightens. "The other girls' fathers. Most of them are shirtless. I think she found them on social media feeds."

I turn to Annie, who's looking at me with big eyes.

"I don't know what kind of lifestyle you support, Mr. Jamieson," the principal goes on stiffly, "but I'm concerned this is unhealthy. We are very particular about the environment we put our children in."

My instinct is to lose my shit but some impulse has me holding it at bay. "Annie, whose father is it?"

"I forget. I put a few of them up."

She's being vague, but the expression on her face is strange. Like she knows the answer but doesn't want to say.

She's not afraid. More like...embarrassed.

This isn't adding up. "Do you..." I clear my throat. "Are you having feelings for other kids' fathers?"

Annie scrunches up her face. "Of course not. They're old. That's weird."

Now I'm more confused. "So why would you do it?"

A light bulb goes on and I swallow the groan.

"Annie," I start, shifting back in my chair, "do any of the other girls have dad photos in their lockers?"

"Yes."

"Whose dad?"

"Mine. And they remind me of it every damned day," she mutters.

"I see."

I nod to the principal, who's looking perplexed.

"Are you punishing the other girls?" I ask.

"But—that's different, Mr. Jamieson."

"How so? Just because I'm in entertainment and the other kids' dads are investment bankers makes it okay for them to tease my kid about me?"

Her mouth tightens. "We do aim to ensure positive and healthy social relationships. But we also have discretion to assign punishment for behavior that doesn't fit our school's values. As a result, Anne will do four weeks' community service filing books at the library every day after school."

Normally I'm all for teachers keeping kids in line, because I think they have too much latitude to get into trouble.

But she picked the wrong day and the wrong kid.

I shift in my seat and I swear her gaze flicks down my body. Over my T-shirt. Hell, maybe it even reaches the jeans but I'm looking at her face.

"Maybe you know how difficult it is to be a single parent, but if you don't, let me help you." I lean across the desk I probably paid for, keeping my voice deliberately measured. "It's really *fucking hard*. I've traveled to sixty countries. But nothing about selling out stadiums or managing media prepares you for the day your kid glues tampons to someone's books. Or comes home with some teenaged Smurf. Or asks you if you think she's a lesbian." I think I hear Annie snort beside me. "But you know what? We do okay.

"Now let me get this straight. You're telling me my honor is threatened and my daughter's crime was defending herself, and me, from a bunch of hormonal teenagers with a thing for thirty-year-old abs. If you try to punish her for that, I will not only put a stop on her tuition checks and take her to the second best school in the city, but I will buy her a pony, an ice cream cake, a damned locker full of tampons and dad pictures and anything else she wants along the way. Do we understand one another?"

The principal stares at me in shock for the better part of a minute before recovering. "Given the gray area of the circumstances, I think we can let this go." She turns to Annie. "But you will stay out of trouble the remainder of the semester."

Annie nods dutifully.

We walk out of the office together and get six steps down the hall before I lean back against the wall, my head hitting the plaster as I shut my eyes.

"Are you okay?" Annie asks tentatively.

My shoulders rock. "You got them back by posting pictures of their dads?"

"Yeah. Some pretty nasty shirtless ones from trips to the Hamptons. They haven't talked about you all week. But I guess they tattled on me." She swipes at her eyes. "You were amazing in there."

My chest tightens until it's hard to breathe. It's the best moment I can remember, and it doesn't have to do with money or lawyers or regret or our past. It's just...

Now.

She glances down at her phone.

"Who's that?"

"Tyler."

Which reminds me. "Haley said you could go to Wicked and play with other kids."

Her eyes light up. "Really?"

"Yeah. No pressure—"

"I'm so there."

14

HALEY

I'm pretty sure heaven is a recording studio rigged up with the best sound mixing software money can buy, plus a little help from DRE when we get stuck.

Oh yeah. And Riot Act, including the one and only Jax Jamieson, on the other side of the glass.

I could live a thousand lifetimes and never get the kind of satisfaction I get from being part of this process. Because now that Jax is in it, he's all in.

It's incredible to watch. The way he writes and rewrites, how his mind turns things over.

I see why Cross didn't want to record without Jax, because he's the spark, the catalyst. He sticks together Kyle's crazy ideas, Brick's bass line, Mace's long quiet periods punctuated with moments of excitement when he jumps on a new idea, spins it out, makes it bigger than before.

I tried to replicate this chemistry in computer programs. Now I see why I can't.

Computers can unpack our logic and build it up better than we ever could. They can beat us at chess, at investing, at planning.

But they can't out-create us. They can't out-feel us.

No one can out-feel Jax when he's like this.

"Come out with me," Jax says at the end of the day Friday on our way to the meeting with Todd. "Annie'll be there too. She killed a test this week, so she gets to pick the restaurant. But she's dying to see you. Since she learned about your program, you're pretty much her hero."

"I heard Mace was her hero."

"Don't tell him he's been replaced." Jax grins. He's so high he's practically flying, and I can't resist smiling. "But seriously. I haven't seen you all week."

"You've seen me every day," I counter.

"Yeah. But that's you and Jerry. Team Jaley. Wait, that could be us. Team Herry." He makes a face. "And even if I get you alone for two seconds, we're surrounded by three other dudes."

"And you need to get me alone because...?"

"Isn't it obvious?" His grin melts me to my core. "I want to do wicked things to you, Wicked girl."

So truth time. Since we hooked up in my office earlier this week, I've been doing my best to act professional. Channel the best parts of my father, the record executive, and bring them to the studio.

But Shannon Cross never had to deal with Jax Jamieson looking at him the way he's looking at me right now.

"I thought we had an ending."

"An ending has multiple parts. This entire album is an ending to my career. It has multiple tracks, multiple verses..." his mouth is hot on my ear. "We could have multiple lots of things."

Shit.

The problem isn't the physical. At least, it isn't only the physical.

It's that I've never been able to hold back with Jax. He's like a storm, tearing through me, leaving me in pieces even when he doesn't mean to.

He can't help it. It's his nature.

But we have other problems.

I shove the personal ones from my mind as we file into the conference room where Todd is already sitting, holding a copy of the file I emailed him not an hour ago.

"What the hell is this?" he asks.

"It's the track listing for the album," I reply, dropping into a seat as Jax takes the next one over.

Todd holds up the sheet. "It's four tracks."

"Right. We're making an EP called *Now*. Have you listened to the tracks? The first two are clear singles. We can release them in a matter of weeks. We've worked up a marketing plan to support this."

"Tell me you're fucking with me. This is what you've been working on for the past month?" He lifts the paper. "We're doing an LP." He turns to Jax, dismissing me as if I'm there to bring them coffee.

Jax opens his mouth to issue a stinging retort, but I lift a hand.

He drops back in his chair, folding his arms over his chest. This is my fight, and I'm grateful he's letting me take it.

"If you read his contract," I start, "it doesn't specify an LP. Now, maybe our lawyers didn't do their job. Or maybe my father, like me, thought it would make sense to make the right album at the right time. Which," I can't help adding, "is an EP."

"What are you now, his lawyer?"

"I'm an owner of this company. And someone who gives a shit how this album turns out." Todd goes red but I don't stop. "Now. Do you want me to tell Derek you're stuck on this idea of making an LP? Because you'll be making it without Jax."

Todd's gaze flicks back to Jax, who looks up from where he's inspecting his nails. He slings an arm over the back of his chair, appearing every bit the artist who'd rather be anywhere but in this meeting, though I'm sure he's smirking on the inside. "She's right. We gotta get back. My kid's got swim camp this summer."

I could hug him.

When Todd shoves out of his chair and stalks out the door, I do.

"He always have that much of a stick up his ass?" Jax asks as we walk back from the conference room side by side.

I hide a smile. "Some days it's higher."

"I dunno what Derek saw in him."

"Track record. He's conservative, has turned out a lot of big albums."

"Least we got the go ahead on the EP."

It's a small win, but it doesn't feel like it.

I wave to Derek's admin, who's packing up for the day. Her gaze flicks from me to Jax.

"Do you think Todd knows?" I venture as we make our way down the hall to my office.

Jax's expression darkens. "What? That I fucked you senseless in your office Tuesday night?"

I flinch, hoping to hell no one overheard. "Yeah, that."

"How would he? I was on my best

behaviour in that meeting. Which, come to think of it, is getting old."

He holds the door to my office for me and I duck through.

I'm barely inside when he spins me around, pressing my back against the wall. I'm breathless before his hips pin mine in place.

"Come for dinner," Jax murmurs.

The offer he's making with his body feels very different than dinner. "And then?"

"And then I'll make you come so hard your toes cramp for a week." He flashes me a boyish smile that has my knees going weak. "Unless you're busy."

"I am meeting someone shortly."

Jax's eyes flash.

The jealousy shouldn't make me happy.

But hey. No one's perfect.

I slip out from between him and the wall and circle my desk, dropping into the chair. "He's kind of amazing. He has blue eyes and blue hair—"

"Tyler." He shakes his head. "What the hell is it with that kid? He's got Annie wrapped around his finger too. I never should've let her do this after school thing… ah well. What do you say?"

My hesitation elicits a frown.

"It's not that I don't want to spend time with you," I start, "it's just… we need to focus on this album. And we said this was an ending…"

"Right."

"…And I don't want to get attached. If you're trying to sleep with me—"

"I'm totally trying to sleep with you." His bluntness doesn't make him any easier to turn down. Not when he's standing so close and wearing that T-shirt that pulls tight over his body and those jeans that fit every part of his lean legs to perfection. "But I also want to spend time with you. I'm not asking for forever. I want to show you I fucked up. That the way we ended things isn't the way I wanted them to end. I'm not that guy, Hales."

My heart's issuing a warning, but he's being so reasonable, it's hard to argue in my head.

When the three of us go out for dinner, Annie picks some vegan place, and over cashew cream bowls, she babbles all about her time in the studio.

"The best part is that no one tells you what

to do or not do," she goes on, her eyes flicking between her food, Jax, and me like a laser pointer. "I've never seen so many guitars before." She shoots me a look. "Hey, Haley. What would happen if one of them got broken? Not me," she protests at her father's rough intake of breath. "I'm just saying."

"Those instruments cost thousands of dollars," he states.

Her eyes widen. "No one's done anything on purpose. But you might want to look at the guitars."

I groan inwardly. If something needs repairs, it's going to come from my pocket.

The reality is, things happen from time to time. They're kids. Things break.

"It's fine, Annie."

She blows out a breath, relieved. "But it's not Tyler," she adds. "Tyler's super careful. And he knows everything."

Jax groans. "I'm sure he doesn't know everything."

"He does. He's so talented. Don't you think so, Haley?"

"He's pretty talented."

Jax shoots me a look, and when Annie goes

back to her food, I can't resist winking at him. Damn, it's cute watching him dad. He was always loving with her, but now there's this extra protectiveness that he's comfortable with, like familiar clothes.

I didn't expect it to be this attractive.

When I'd learned I was pregnant, a lot of emotions had washed over me. Denial. Terror.

Eventually, possibility.

Some small part of me had hoped that it might be a reason for us to figure things out.

Which I know now was naïve.

Before the miscarriage, I'd come round to the idea of being a single mom. I had enough to provide for two between my earnings working with Carter and my inheritance.

When it happened, I hadn't expected the pang of loss, the mourning. But there it was. It took months before I got my head on straight.

Now, seeing Jax with Annie? It's like all the emotions, all the possibilities, rush back.

"You guys gang up on me," Jax murmurs when Annie goes to the bathroom, taking a long drink of water.

I find a smile. "It's girl talk."

"Girl talk. You mean about boys."

I snort. “Newsflash. Girls talk about things other than the opposite sex. We talk about dreams. Fears. Failures. The future. Things guys never talk about.”

He turns that over. “Sounds scary.”

“The alternative scares me more. That you can spend all the time without talking about it.” I take a sip of my drink. “‘You can live a hundred years without really living a minute’.”

“More Kierkegaard?”

I love that he remembers. “Close. Gilmore Girls.” He laughs. “My mom and I used to watch it. I have a feeling Annie would like it too.”

“Hales?” Jax’s expression shifts and there’s an intensity that steals my breath. “Sometimes guys think about those things.”

My hand tightens on the water glass, the icy sweat making my grip slippier, because suddenly I’m thinking about those things with him.

We have more in common now than ever, given my work at Wicked, and I love talking with him, hanging out with him.

But even though I’d probably survive

having my heart broken by Jax a second time, I'm not ready to line up for it.

I finish my food and set down my fork. "You ever talk to Grace?"

"We're on the outs since I won custody. Annie sees her on holidays. Every few weeks in between. Though my sister wasn't thrilled with the idea of us coming to Philly for a couple of months."

"She must miss Annie so much. It's too bad you guys couldn't come to an agreement."

He cuts a piece of his food, eats it. "The judge is checking in in a year. If Grace's situation has stabilized..." he trails off.

"There's still a chance the arrangement could change?"

He shifts. "There's always a chance things could change."

And there it is. No matter how much we control life, there will always be uncertainty.

Annie returns, dropping into her chair. "Are you coming over, Haley? You can. It's totally fine." Her intelligent eyes focus on me.

I glance toward Jax, but he's grabbed the bill. He's busy paying it, or acting as if he's not listening.

Annie leans in. "If it helps, my dad never has people over."

He blinks at her a moment before dissolving into a huge grin that has my chest squeezing.

"Okay," I agree. "For a little while."

We drive back to his place together and go up the elevator.

"It's after ten and a school night. Bedtime, squirt."

She salutes with an eye roll and closes her door.

"You've raised quite the kid."

"Before tonight, I can't remember her calling me her dad."

"Really?" A bubble of emotion rises up in my chest.

"Yeah." He goes to the kitchen and pours two bourbons. He passes one to me. "Remember the first time we drank this together? Because I sure do."

Jax's knowing look has me squirming. "I think I stripped in your foyer. It was mortifying."

"You had me the second I opened the door," he says, solemn.

"You still owe me. I always feel vulnerable in front of you."

Jax cocks his head, considering. Then he reaches for my phone on the counter.

My breath catches even before he hooks a finger in the waist of my skirt. "I'll make it up to you."

He tugs me into his bedroom. It's not so different from the one in Dallas, but it's more homey looking. Like someone picked out the individual elements. But the décor is the last thing on my mind when he scrolls through my phone and puts on a song.

My eyes widen.

"I was holding that for a friend," I protest as the opening chords of "I Love Rock 'n' Roll" play.

"Uh-huh." He points at the end of the bed. "Sit."

I do.

He takes two steps back, his gaze locked with mine. I have no idea what's happening and I'm about to ask when his next movement stuns me silent.

Jax Jamieson reaches for the hem of his shirt.

And, with a wicked gleam in his eye, he strips.

I don't know if it's the sight of his abs or the bourbon coursing through me that's responsible for the wave of light-headedness.

Maybe both.

I dissolve into laughter, trying to keep my voice down since Annie's across the hall.

He peels the shirt over his head and tosses it at me. I catch it. "Pretty soon I'm going to have more of your clothes than you do," I murmur.

Jax winks at me. "I don't think so, babysitter."

I couldn't have pictured Jax from two years ago doing this. He took himself way too seriously.

I'm cracking up and so turned on at the same time, and I had no idea before this moment that was even possible.

I lean back, content to watch the show.

When his hands go to the button of his jeans, I swallow.

He works the button free. Then the zipper.

"You slowed down," I complain, breathy.

"It's called a striptease for a reason,

Hales." But his warm voice is tinged with roughness too, as if he likes watching me watch him.

I try and fail to hold in the moan as he works his pants off and steps closer to me.

"What's wrong," he prods, the smug grin never leaving his face.

My gaze tries to take all of him in. His broad chest, hard shoulders, rippling abs, muscled legs. The outline of his obvious erection through his shorts.

"How are you still so fucking hot," I mumble.

Some of the smugness fades as he bends over, pressing a scorching kiss on my startled mouth.

"You want to do the honors?" he asks when he pulls back, glancing at his shorts.

"I feel like I need dollar bills."

"Hales," Jax says evenly, "I'm a zillionaire. You're going to have to do better than that."

He's ridiculous, and I love it. Handsome and playful and totally irresistible. I love how his hair falls over his face. How he smells, tastes. The feel of his skin, smooth over muscles, under my hands.

I pull down the waistband an inch at a time.

He's hard and thick and perfect and eye level, and my mouth waters just looking at him.

"Can I tell you something?" I whisper.

"What."

"I never blew anyone before you."

The humor falls away, replaced with heat and something else. "Seriously?"

I shake my head. "I mean, I've watched people do it in porn. Even read up on how to do it, in case I wanted to someday." I flush. "But I never wanted to before."

"You're telling me you lost your oral virginity out of spite?"

"Yes. And it was totally worth it."

I reach for his cock, shifting forward because all I want is to lick him but he pushes me back on the bed.

"That's not how this works."

"No?" I prop myself up on my elbows, breathless and turned on and a little exasperated at being denied. "Fine. Go on and mansplain it to me, Jax."

But my irritation doesn't bother him a bit. He reaches for my skirt, and I'm glad it's stretchy because he manages to strip it down my hips without lifting me off the bed. My shirt comes next.

Jax's gaze darkens with appreciation as he takes in the soft pink lace-covered bra and panties.

"How this works is you lie on that bed and let me worship you."

Okay, well that doesn't sound terrible.

Even though he says it like it's way more than sex.

Especially since he does.

Jax drops to his knees, and my exhale trembles through my lips.

"The first time we did this," he says, his voice a rasp, "I told you the value of my songs." I swallow the laugh at the memory. "It's not my go-to line, but man, it got you wet."

His grin fades and I realize that even on his knees, he's no less strong, no less compelling. I would do anything he asked.

"Should've known then you'd choose Wicked over me."

The moment of seriousness has me swallowing. "I wanted you both. I wanted it all." I reach toward him, running a hand through his hair.

His breath is warm on my stomach as he closes in. "What if you could have it all? Not for forever," he says before I can protest that it's impossible. "For now."

If there's one thing I've learned in the past two years, it's that life takes you on a ride. You need to fight for what you believe in, but you also need to be prepared to have it all ripped away at any second.

My hands fist in the comforter because I know I'm not going to stop him tonight. I want to give him everything he wants.

"Okay," I whisper, and I swear his eyes change color. "What are you waiting for, Jax Jamieson? Rock my fucking world."

He tugs my panties down and I lift my hips, his amber gaze never leaving mine.

His mouth drops. He presses a kiss to the inside of my thigh and I shiver.

Then he licks a fiery line from my core up over my clit.

I grab his hair on an ugly noise that's half moan, half protest.

Because *shit*, that's intense. It's as if he's

inside me in a whole new way, and I can't hide anything from him like this.

I'm so tempted to stop him.

"Damn, you're beautiful," he murmurs against my slick skin.

I force myself to relax my hold and squeeze my eyes shut.

Every inch of me's feeling his lips, his tongue. The way he plays me as if I'm his instrument and he's the best in the world.

After a minute, it's starting to feel good.

"OhmigodJaaax..."

The comforter scratches my bare back and I arch to get away from it, closer to him.

When his fingers join in, pressing deep inside me, I think I hit the ceiling.

Jax pulls back to shift up my body. "I love how you taste," he murmurs. "I can't believe I've been without it my whole life." Then he kisses me, and I taste myself. It shouldn't be so hot, but it is.

When he drops back down my body, his lips, his tongue, his hands, work together in such beautiful concert I can't speak. Can't breathe. Can't do anything but exist in complete and utter awe of him and the way he makes me feel.

He drags me up the cliff, to the edge. When I'm hovering on it, gasping, grabbing at his hair, he waits a long moment, as if to imprint in my mind the fact that he brought me there.

Then he shoves me off it.

I bite my cheek to keep from screaming as wave after wave of pure sensation tears through me.

Jax's real magic is that he blows my mind utterly, completely, then the next second he makes me forget there's ever been any other way.

As I struggle to catch my breath, winded and wrecked and staring at the dimmed overhead light, I wonder if that was his plan all along.

15

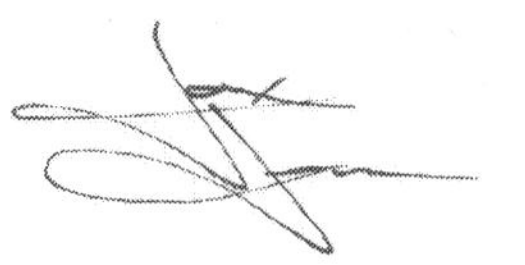

"Is that real?" Tyler hefts the Grammy, weighing it.

"It's papier-mâché."

The door opens, and Haley sticks her head into the conference room. "You're late for your interview—whoa. What's going on?"

I glance around the room, which is lined with glass cases and awards.

"Show and tell. Light some fires under some asses. I figured there was enough memorabilia at Wicked, but Annie wanted to do it. So I had some stuff packed up and shipped here."

Haley looks around the room in amazement at the stacks of instruments, photos, and awards covering the long table and arranged around the outside of the room. "Wow. I'm surprised you wanted to dust all this off. I thought it might bring back bad memories."

I shrug. "Not a big deal. The kids are having fun."

Annie's showing some of my old costumes to the other kids.

"Can I put this on?" Tyler holds up the logo T-shirt and a pair of leather pants from my first tour.

"The jacket, sure. Not the pants. That's crossing a line." I turn back to Haley. "You gonna bust me for taking a break, boss?"

"I guess not."

I steer her to the back corner of the room. Chords start up as one of the kids grabs my guitar.

Her eyes fly wide. "Is that your—"

"It's just my old Telecaster, it's fine." I take in her expression. "But something's wrong."

"It's this interview you're doing. I didn't expect you to have to go through the media circus to make this album."

I brush a thumb over her cheek.

"You know I've been doing these since you were Annie's age."

Haley sighs out a breath. “I know.”

But it’s cute that she’s worried about me.

A lot of things she does are cute. The ones that aren’t are either frustrating—like when she argues with me over a track, or the lunch order, or whether I can touch her when we’re both bent over the soundboard together—or completely intoxicating.

Three nights ago, we went for dinner with Annie. Haley came over after.

And *stayed over*.

It wasn’t just sex, though holy shit was that insane. The things she let me do to her, the things she wanted to do to me… on paper I’ve done it all before but it’s never been like that.

It’s never *meant* that.

I knew it while I was getting her off with my tongue, feeling her body tight everywhere. When I was stroking inside her, our sweat mingling, telling myself to hold out for one more minute so I could see her fall apart.

Afterward, I’d held her in my arms as we stayed up all night talking and laughing and teasing.

It’s getting harder to admit this is part of

our ending. I want to take our three minute song and make it four, or five.

We leave the kids in the room—I'd told Annie to keep an eye on things, not that I'm worried about it really—and start down the hall toward the elevator.

"I heard you were recording with the kids yesterday," she says as I hit the button for G and the doors close.

"It was fun. Tyler's got something."

She smiles. "I know he does."

The doors open and we cross the lobby.

"Cross started this program. In the past two years, I've taken it up a notch. Now they get experience mixing, producing. I borrow time from the marketing team to talk about how to sell the music. From anyone who'll help."

Haley follows me out into the sunlight, slipping on sunglasses, and to the Acura. I hit the locks and grab the passenger door so she can shift inside.

I round to the driver's side, then I take my seat and turn on the engine.

"I'll help."

Her eyes widen. "Really?"

"Any way I can. In the past month, it feels

like you helped me get my kid back, Hales. And my music." I swallow the emotion rising up. "I know I wasn't the easiest to convince, but I'm stubborn like that."

"Sometimes we both are," she says softly.

I force my attention to the road as we navigate the heavy traffic to the studio.

For the past two weeks, we've been busy with the album.

I've also sat in on two sessions with the kids.

They're talented, and I know Haley's really into it.

What I didn't expect was for me to be into it. I like watching them mess around and screw up and try new things. I learn from them, too. It's a different way to do music than I ever thought of.

Given what I've been through, the ups and downs, I can mentor them, be with them, see the world through their eyes. It makes me feel like maybe I didn't screw everything up. Like maybe the unpredictable roller coaster I lived can help *them* live.

We get there, park, and go inside.

The interview I'm about to do is for

national television, but they'll record here and broadcast across a bunch of networks.

Serena's waiting to greet us at the soundstage… with Todd.

"Run out of real work to do?" I drawl as he looks between us.

"Just came to supervise the company's investment." He turns away, getting on his phone, and I watch him wander the edge of the studio like a dark shadow.

Serena introduces me to the host while I get mic'd up. I take a seat on the stool—why these places have dumb little stools, I have no idea—and we get a countdown.

When it reaches zero, the female host with the big TV smile accosts me. "Jax Jamieson is back, world. And he and Riot Act are doing a new album. Why now?"

It's best to stick close to the truth with media. "I wasn't sure I had something left to give. Someone convinced me I was wrong."

"Aren't we glad they did? You retired for two years and did cologne commercials."

"I did *one* cologne commercial," I correct, raising a brow.

"It's good to have you back. When's the tour?"

I swallow my surprise. I know better than to outright deny something, just as I know better than to prop it up. I keep my voice level as I say, "I'm focusing on my family right now. My daughter."

"Her mother's not in the picture?"

"No."

"I think I heard a thousand ovaries break across America. You heard it here first, ladies. Jax Jamieson is unattached."

"Actually," I say, not sure why it bothers me to hear her say that, "that's not true. Outside of my family, there's only one girl who's ever had my heart."

Her eyes gleam like she's just spotted a hundred dollar bill stuck to her designer shoe. "Who's the lucky woman and what did she do to land you?"

I search for Haley across the room, find her gaze.

"She yelled at me, and hit me, and then followed me around for months."

Her jaw drops, and she's shaking her head, tightly.

"She sang my songs even when I told her not to. She kept all my secrets and pretty much showed me how to live again."

The head shaking stops as Haley's eyes glass over. My chest tightens as I swallow the grin.

"So the way to your heart is through stalking?" the host asks, bringing me back.

"Nah, so please don't try it. This particular version of stalking can't be replicated. It was a onetime deal. I read it as charming. It should've been weird as fuck."

"Wow. Okay then. We're playing the first official clip of a song from Riot Act."

I take off my mic and feel eyes on me. Not Haley's—she's pulled into a conversation with Serena. The head of production.

This is not the kind of inconspicuous I promised to be.

Todd shoves his hands in his pockets, spanning the distance between us in a few strides. "Are you trying to start a rumor? Or you just know how to leave them wanting more?"

"That's my job."

The album's nearly done. Working these crazy long days has been good for me, done something for me, being back in the studio feels like it's changing me in other ways. Besides that I wear more jeans—which delights Annie to no end—it feels like my brain's getting back on some track I didn't know I'd jumped.

"It's interesting." Todd's gaze lands on Haley as she exchanges a few words with the host, and I wonder how long I've been staring.

"What is."

"Wicked tried to contact you for months. Then she calls and you come running."

He's trying to bait me, and I force myself to stay easygoing. "Apparently she asked the right question."

I turn away from him and Serena catches my eye. "Jax, can I talk to you about promotion?"

She walks me to one end of the stage while Todd stalks toward the door. She sighs when he leaves. "There's something you need to know. If the album's not a success, Haley's program will get cut. I'm telling you because she won't put that pressure on you, but I want you to know that what you're doing here matters."

As Serena goes to meet her friend, a stone settles in my stomach.

When Haley called me back here, she made a play for my soul. For the man she knows I can be.

She took that chance on me.

Not in the past.

Right now. Despite how things ended last time. Despite how I treated her, and everything she's been through.

Which makes it that much harder to remind myself this is all part of our ending.

16

HALEY

Two months ago I wouldn't have believed it was possible.

That Jax would come back. That he'd record the kind of songs that leave me breathless. That we'd save the program.

But when the album drops, it drops with a bang.

"No matter what Kyle says, the cake is not that bad," Serena prods. "It's a party. Look happier. The critics giving early reviews have said it's good, but we both know it anyway. The first single's getting airplay. This is what people want."

"I know."

This party has an entirely different vibe

than Jerry's retirement party. This one's small. Private. Personal.

It's not five hundred people.

It's not even fifty.

It includes the band. A few other artists. The staff at the studio. The kids, at Jax's suggestion.

My gaze lands on Tyler, who's laughing with Annie and some of the others.

Serena and the entire PR team have been promoting their asses off. I hope it's enough.

"You in a sugar coma?"

I turn to find Jax behind me, looking gorgeous in faded jeans, white sneakers and a Pink Floyd T-shirt. "There you are. I'm surprised you made it with all the interviews you're doing."

He shrugs. "Might as well get as much publicity as we can."

"Jax, no matter what happens? This album is amazing."

A grin takes over his handsome face. "It's not bad."

Over the past two weeks, he's been working his ass off to get this album finished and mixed. The whole band has.

I don't know why he's started doubling down, but I appreciate it.

The first track was a love song that went down easy.

The second, about growing pains, stuck a little.

The third was about taking your time.

The fourth...

The fourth, called "Line of Sight," was about changing perspectives. Seeing things in new ways.

I never expected to like another song more than the one Jax wrote two years ago and left on the floor of a diner, but I love this one.

Recording it was bittersweet, because I didn't want it to be over.

And maybe he didn't either.

I've gotten used to working next to him again in the studio during the day. It's amazing how fast the old pattern came back, even though we were only on tour for a month. Sometimes I think it was the best month of my life.

Todd's been lurking over us the whole time, so we've been keeping it strictly professional.

But Jax would text me, tease me. We'd exchange secret smiles and laughter.

I don't want anyone getting the wrong idea about why he's here.

Because why we're here is to make this album. Not to see if there's some kind of second chance for us.

Jax and I haven't talked about what would happen when the album is finished because we both know there's an expiration date on this.

We each have responsibilities. You could say we didn't choose them, but we did. Jax found Annie, and he decided to be there for her. I chose this program, these kids, even when it was hard.

The door opens, and we all turn toward it.

Derek's there, with Todd in tow. "We have the numbers. The album's gone gold. At this rate, it should hit platinum by next weekend."

The room erupt with cheers.

I throw my arms around Jax's neck, burying my face in his shoulder in delight. "Oh my God. Jax...you have no idea how much this means."

"I think I do." He pulls back. His face isn't quite a reflection of the ecstasy in mine, but it's close. “Serena told me you bet the program on this.”

Apprehension starts up in my gut as I scan his expression. “Are you mad?”

“No. It means a lot that you have that kind of faith in me. I’m glad you dragged me back here. I needed this.”

“Me too.”

Something deeper in his gaze makes my heart kick in my chest. Because he’s right.

Derek interrupts my daydream. “Haley. A word.”

I tear my gaze from Jax and follow Derek out to the hall, shutting the door after us.

The sounds of the party all but disappear.

Thank you, soundproofing.

“So I guess the program is saved.”

His mouth is a stern line. “About that. Something went missing from a rehearsal room a few weeks back. The one where your kids practice.”

My smile fades a little. “A lot of people practice there.”

“A lot of people are professional musicians,” Todd states. “And the rest are children who wouldn't think twice about selling a guitar."

My minds works to connect the dots.

"In light of this violation," Derek interjects, "I can't in good conscience recommend we pursue your program."

I hold up a hand. "It's a misunderstanding. None of my kids would do that. If you don't believe their reputation, believe mine. I have never done anything to compromise my personal integrity or this company's."

Todd lets out a skeptical sound. "Your reputation is worth less than it used to be."

I fold my arms over my chest, not bothering for once to hide my resentment. This guy has taken enough of my time and patience and for a second I wish I still had control of the company so I could fire his arrogant ass. "What the hell is that supposed to mean?"

But instead of rising to the bait, he smirks. "As you know, there's a security camera in each studio. We were searching the footage. The angle doesn't show the instrument that went missing, but we did find something very interesting."

The tone of his voice has alarm bells going

off in my head. I have no idea what he might have found, so why the hell is he being—

My eyes fall shut.

Me blowing Jax.

He doesn't have to say it.

Every part of me's boiling with humiliation and indignation. But I force my chin up.

"Derek, I swear to God—"

His face lines with regret. "I understand you're upset, and I assure you, we will destroy the footage. But we also need to make a decision about the program."

"You can't force me out of the company."

"No. But the majority shareholders have been onside with the idea of cutting the program for two months, even before this latest incident." The conflicted expression on his face doesn't make his words easier to digest. "It's done, Haley. We can give you two weeks to wrap things up."

It's done. The phrase echoes in my brain as he leaves.

It takes me a moment to realize Todd's lingered behind.

"I'll go somewhere else to run the program," I state. "We'll take what we've started and find a new home."

He smirks. "You really will be starting over. The recordings are company property. Every song those kids have laid down since this program started. It's all in the legal agreement they sign when they walk in the door."

I feel myself go pale.

How I find my way to my office, I have no idea. But I'm sitting on my desk, swiping at angry tears when Jax's voice interrupts me.

"Hales." I look up to meet his concerned gaze. "What happened?"

"They're cutting the program. The album's a huge success, and they're cutting it anyway." I hate how my voice sounds. I hate feeling weak.

Jax's body stiffens, his gaze jerking toward the hallway. "Was this Derek or that prick Todd?"

"I'll figure it out. You've done more than enough." I manage a watery smile. "I dragged you and your daughter across the country on a week's notice to write and record all new original material. Your work here is done. You paid me back by delivering a platinum album."

"I hope that's not all I delivered." The

warmth in his tone has me thinking about everything that's happened between us.

He drops onto the desk next to me, toeing the carpet as he shoves his hands in his pockets.

If someone told me we'd have another shot at an ending, I'd have called them crazy. But we have had, and it's been beautiful.

Jax's album is complete. In some ways, this is the culmination of what I wanted when I took over Wicked from Cross.

I wanted to find another Jax.

I did. I found it in him, when he didn't think it was there.

I swallow the lump in my throat. "Three years ago, all I wanted was to matter. I wanted you to teach me how, and you did." I rest a hand on the denim covering his thigh as emotions roll over me in waves. "You did, and I'm so grateful."

My gaze lifts to his. He turns my words over in his mind. "That's nothing, Hales. You helped me get my kid back in a way the lawyers couldn't. And my music."

It takes everything in me just to breathe

right now. To tell my body that everything's the way it's supposed to be.

Because I just lost my program, and it feels as if I'm about to lose something that matters even more.

I squeeze his hand, looking past him to the Ireland picture.

"I always liked that one," he says, as if he can read my mind.

"Me too. Do you ever miss him?"

"Cross?" I expect him to laugh, but he just looks around the office. "Sometimes. He gave me someone to blame, and blaming is easier. You can't push against the world when there's no one to resist."

"The first time I came to this office after learning Cross was my father, he gave me shit for asking bad questions. Said there was one question I should be asking, and if I knew what it was, I'd know him better."

"And?"

"The question is why he sent me on tour with you."

Jax's gaze scans mine. "You wish he was still here so you could ask him?"

I shake my head. "I don't need to ask him. I know."

Somehow a piece of hair slipped into my face, and I tuck it back before turning toward him.

"I was the daughter he didn't know what to do with. You were the son he could never ask for. And as much as he fucked up… I think he knew we'd be good for each other, Jax."

Jax shifts off the desk and steps between my legs, tilting his face toward mine. His touch is comforting on my thighs.

I was holding it together until this moment, but when his mouth grazes mine once, twice, my arms wrap around him and hold him against me. Every ounce of emotion and need pouring out of him is destroying me, and I lose myself in the kiss.

I hate the idea of not having him next to me in the morning, not being around him, not sharing his smiles and his moods.

We break apart, breathing heavily.

"When are you going back to Dallas?"

"This weekend."

I nod, but it's mechanical.

"It doesn't mean we can't be friends, Hales,"

he murmurs, the words spilling into one another in a very un-Jax-like way. "I want you to call me. I swear to God I'll answer. Not just if you're pregnant. But of course then too." I hiccup a laugh. "If you have a bad day. Hell, a good one. I want to know. Promise me."

Nodding is easier than speaking, but Jax waits until I find my voice. "I promise," I whisper.

I wait until he's retreated to the hall before I close the door quietly and let the tears stream down my face.

17

The next few days feel like I'm going through the motions. Finishing media that suddenly feels pointless. Fending off offers from my agent, which are exploding now that I have a new album. Calling my housekeeper to make sure everything's set for when I get back. Packing up my clothes, both the T-shirts and the preppy ones.

Endings always suck, and I can't decide which are worse. The kind where you're ripped apart, where nothing but evil forces could keep you separated?

Or the kind that happens when you're an adult and you have to walk away on your own steam.

Definitely that one.

"I'm sad you're leaving." The boy's murmured voice has me glancing in the rearview mirror.

"Me too," Annie says back.

I clear my throat. "We're almost at Tyler's house."

"Can we drive around a little more?" Annie pleads.

Two pairs of eyes find mine in the mirror.

They're kids. It shouldn't get to me.

Except it's like stomping on my soul that's already beaten and bloody.

"Ten more minutes," I say.

They continue to talk in the back, quietly with little bursts of laughter thrown in. Like they'll never get to talk again, even though something tells me they'll be texting every night for weeks.

If someone had told me three months ago we'd get this comfortable in Philly, I'd have called them out on it.

But I like seeing my old band mates. Driving around town in my rental that's almost as familiar as my Bentley.

Annie's even settled in at school.

I slow the car when I realize whose neighborhood we're in. Big houses watch over the street, tucked behind trees older than me and the kids put together.

I notice the sign before the house, and I hit the brakes. "What the fuck..."

"What's wrong?" Annie chirps from the back seat, suddenly alert.

I pull over and start to dial her number, then I change my mind and hit another.

"Hello, this is Serena."

"Her house is for sale. Why."

Annie and Tyler are looking on now.

"Jax." She blows out a breath. "We really have to stop meeting like this."

"Tell me."

"She's been thinking about it for awhile. I guess she decided it was time to make a change."

Time to make a change.

The sign seems to taunt me, which is fucking weird, because I'm not in the habit of hearing voices from dead guy's Victorian mansions.

I've been thinking about what she said about Cross bringing us together.

Now, she's leaving the company. Selling the house.

It's like she's shedding the last part of him, which shouldn't bug me because God knows I wasn't the guy's biggest fan.

But it feels more final than our ending, like she's erasing the past somehow. I'm not just losing her, I'm losing what brought us together. Our common ground, and I'm just sitting here staring at the damned sign like a moron.

I need to be back in Dallas. Not just because of Annie. Because that's what I chose. It's my life.

But I've spent a lot of time beating myself up for what I should do.

Resolve sets in. "Get her to take the house off the market. Say whatever you have to. That your rat infested the attic with rabies. I don't care. And I want a meeting. Now. The band. Lita. You. No Haley."

I hang up.

"What's going on?" Annie asks.

"Change of plans." I wheel the car around.

18

HALEY

When I enter Carter's office, it's the same as I remember it, plus a few new awards. The walls are covered in obscure-looking equations and comic book covers. It's perfect for him. He's a genius who refuses to grow up.

"I have an idea for a new project," I say.

I explain it to him. He listens, raising a brow on his unusually tan face.

When I finish, my former professor's eyes sparkle. "What happened to Mr. Teenager-bait Musician?"

I shouldn't be surprised he knows about Jax. "He was here to cut an album. It's over."

Jax left two weeks ago.

Fifteen days if you're counting.

We've texted a bit but he's been especially vague about his activities since returning to Dallas. And neither of us has suggested talking on the phone.

Probably because he gets, like I do, that we can't continue the way we were here. There's a new normal and we need to respect that if we're going to move forward with our lives.

I keep telling myself it's going to be fine, but I miss having him here, smelling him, laughing with him, lying next to him.

"Carter, if you're gunning to be my rebound, I'm flattered. But it's not going to happen. Business only."

He shrugs. "Fine. I've been in Costa Rica for the last six weeks. Might go back. I don't need some kid hanging all over me."

I know he's joking about the last part. "You've been there six weeks?"

"Never even noticed, did you?" He smirks. "The beauty of the internet. School semester wrapped in April, which means if I'm not teaching, I can work anywhere. Should've tried it ages ago."

We hash out a plan for the app on his

whiteboard, and I confirm when I can code the first part by.

"Huh. You really are done with your other life."

The words hit me. My other life.

Is that what it'll feel like in a few months? That it was another lifetime? The thought makes my chest ache.

I leave Carter's office and walk around. Campus is quiet, but a few students are chatting along the paths, on the benches. I could've been one of them.

I still can. I can do anything I want.

I'm keeping my shares in the company. But I'm done working at Wicked.

On the way home, I call Serena. "Hey. Do you want to hang out tonight?"

"I'd love to, but I need to work late." My friend sounds strange, as if maybe she feels badly that she's still all-in at Wicked when I'm trying to move on.

"Sure, no problem." I swing in the doors of the house.

"I do need a coffee break though. So talk to me. Any offers on the house?"

I hear her chair creak in the background and picture her going to the kitchen for java.

"Yes, finally." I think of the FOR SALE sign in the driveway. I don't need five thousand square feet of Century-home luxury and I've been meaning to list the house for months. It finally feels like the right time. "We wondered why it was taking so long but my realtor found this blog post about the house being haunted. Apparently that sparked interest like crazy."

"Huh." She sounds far away. "Perfect. Listen. How are you doing with the whole Jax leaving thing?"

I blow out a breath. "It sucks," I say honestly. "I'm trying to focus on a new program with Carter, then I pull out my phone and start typing some emotional text to Jax. I can't send them because we agreed we'd be grownups about this." I sigh out a breath. "Just tell me one thing. Are we still getting messages about the album?"

"It's insane," she replies immediately. "Everyone's connecting to it, feeling it. I mean, come on. It went platinum."

I feel the weight on my shoulders lift a little. "I don't care about that part, Serena. I'm just so glad he made it. That it matters to people."

I don't know if it's my words or the wistfulness in my voice that has her concerned. "Haley, maybe we should talk. I can duck out of work in an hour or so—"

"No, it's fine. Seriously. But can I borrow Scrunchie tonight?"

"Of course. And we're on for lunch tomorrow."

"Wouldn't miss it."

I pick up Scrunchie using my spare key for Serena's apartment and take him home.

Then I curl up on the couch, stick in my earbuds and hit Play on the album I've been waiting to listen to like this.

To feel.

To remember.

I've listened to these tracks hundreds of times. Spent hours tweaking them. Now, Jax's voice seducing me through the headphones is pure catharsis.

"The ground under your feet shifts with everyone you meet

You have a choice, a chance

To keep it all and curse your fate

Tell yourself it's all too late

Keep counting wrongs until they're right or find a new line of sight."

Tears roll down my cheeks through my eyelids. Not because I'm sad.

Because I'm happy.

I'm so fucking happy he made this for the world.

Made it for *me*.

For all of us.

Scrunchie sniffs my neck in support.

After awhile, I force myself to open my notebook computer and go through emails.

Tomorrow's my last official day at Wicked. I need to turn in my pass, and clean out my office.

I scroll through the emails, Scrunchie shifting under my hand as I stroke his soft back.

Maybe I need a skunk.

An email comes in from Tyler asking about our last day in studio. I think of his bright future, snuffed out by Wicked's failing.

I had to tell the kids this week that the program's cut. I didn't tell them that the recordings are Wicked's property.

Now, hearing Jax's album, that seems like the bigger crime.

An idea comes to me.

You can't make him Jax, a voice says. *But you can protect his work. His voice.*

Shifting upright so fast I almost dump Scrunchie from my lap, I dig out the contact list from our board of directors materials.

Then I reach for my phone.

19

HALEY

Last night I slept with Scrunchie in my bed. I like to think it fortified me for the day ahead.

I get up and shower, then I pull on my battle gear.

Jeff gives me a double take as I sweep in the front doors. “Morning, Miss Telfer.”

“Morning, Jeff.” I hitch the empty box on my hip, my Converse sneakers silent on the carpet.

Upstairs, I clean out the office, giving instructions to a man from a moving company on how to care for my father’s art.

“You can’t take that.”

A cold voice has me looking toward the door. "Excuse me?"

Todd sneers. "That's company property."

"It's my father's."

"Shannon Cross would've driven this company into the ground if he'd been here longer. His death—and you selling out—were the best things to happen to Wicked in its history."

I lift the picture and hold it against my chest like a shield. "I didn't realize you knew him."

"He had a chance to hire me. He didn't."

I lower the picture as understanding dawns. "Can I give you some advice, Todd?" I don't wait for him to respond. "Getting revenge on a dead man is hard. Getting anything from a dead man is hard. Respect. Love. Attention. If that's all you want out of life, you'll be waiting a long time."

His gaze narrows, and I lay the frame carefully on the desk.

I lift the file I brought then nestle it under my arm.

I feel Todd on my heels as I pass through

the familiar halls down to Derek's office, where I knock before opening the door.

He's on a call and stares at me as I grab the handset from him. "Sorry. This will only take a second, Derek will call you right back." I hang up.

"Haley. What the hell?"

He shifts back in his chair.

"I have something for you to sign. My lawyer drew these up." I set the file in front of him. "The rights to the recordings and files from the after-school program."

His brows rise. "I didn't realize this was on your mind." He flips through the pages. "We need to put this by the board."

"I already did. I circulated the proposal by email yesterday and got sign-offs from the other major shareholders."

His confusion grows. "So if they've signed off, this is a formality?"

"It's done, Derek," I say, relishing the words a bit too much. "But I thought I'd give you the respect of asking for your signature as CEO."

Todd grunts. "You can't take those. That's years worth of recordings. Terabytes of data."

I glance over my shoulder, acknowledging him for the first time. "What I'm paying for the rights to those recordings is more than fair. Especially considering you called them worthless."

And it is. In fact, it'll be the proceeds from the sale of my house.

Derek signs and I close the folder with a smile. "Gentlemen. I'll see you in the next board meeting."

I stride back down the hall to my office. At the computer I'm about to leave, I double-check that all the relevant files have been uploaded, as I requested from IT, and removed from Wicked's file system.

A feeling of satisfaction works through me. Everything the kids created in that studio since the program's inception is mine.

In legal terms only.

Really, it's theirs.

"Haley!" Serena calls from a window as I take my boxes out to my car. I load my car and wait until she comes down, out of breath. "Damn, running isn't as good for me as it's supposed to be."

"Am I late for lunch?"

"No. You're right on time."

"Good. Because after, I'm going on a little trip."

"Where?"

"Dallas." I grin. "I need to tell Jax something, and it's better in person."

A strange look crosses her face. "Fine. But after lunch." She trots in front of me, and I follow her around the building.

"Where are we going?" I call after her.

Serena stops in front of a massive bus that has me freezing in my tracks.

"Why is Jax's bus here." The doors are open, and my friend's acting like I didn't just ask a question. "Serena..."

Before I can find words, a form appears in the doorway.

Jeans.

A tight T-shirt.

Messy hair.

Amber eyes that stop my heart when they find me. "Hi, Hales."

Jax.

I try to say the word, but all I can manage is to keep breathing.

Being around him has that effect on me, whether I haven't seen him in days or years.

Finally, enough synapses fire to create language.

"What are you doing here?"

"Apparently I bought this years ago. It's how I kept other people off it."

"Don't tell me you blew through your money already and have to tour again."

"Not quite. I did have some ideas for how to spend my retirement, though."

He invites me onto the bus, and with only a moment's hesitation, I follow him up the stairs. My jaw drops.

The living room has been redone. Instead of dark maroon, it's white with bright colors. He leads me through where the curtain used to be. Now, it's a clear door.

"What the..." His couch and other furniture is gone. In its place, equipment. Instruments. "It's a studio?"

"Yup. On wheels."

"But how did you—"

"Acoustics? Jerry helped spec it out. We

redid the interior." He pats the inside wall. "Put on a few layers of absorption materials. Keeps outside noise out and all the good stuff in. I finally got to put those home reno skills to good use."

I can barely take it all in. "It's amazing, don't get me wrong, but why did you do this?"

He grabs my hand. I try to ignore the tingling as I wrap my fingers tighter in his. He pulls me back to the front of the bus, where Serena's leaning against the wall with a dopey expression on her face.

"You didn't notice the pictures?" he asks.

Now I do.

They're the ones from the studio, of the kids. Intermingled with ones from Jax's tours. On stage, and on the road. Images of Jerry, Lita, Mace, Kyle, Brick, Nina, me. Even one of Cross.

My gaze catches on a plaque at the front, and I run a hand over it. "'Big Leap Studio,'" I read under my breath.

"Now we can take it to kids at any school."

"Wait—what do you mean we?"

His eyes gleam. "Come on. You didn't think I'd let you produce without me? Jerry wants a proper retirement, and you can't supervise a dozen junior high students alone."

"You're staying?"

Jax nods, and my breath sticks in my throat. "Here, Dallas, it doesn't matter anymore. I'm tired of doing what I decided I wanted years ago. Because I don't need to lock myself away. Everything we've done here has made me realize I have choices. I always have, even if it didn't feel that way." Tingles run up my arm and I glance down to see him rubbing a circle in my palm. "Annie's on board, and Grace has agreed to a schedule of sharing time. Because I need my kid, but I also need you, Hales. I love the shit out of you. I think it started the night you got my phone back. Or maybe when you told me I was second best to Leonard Cohen." His dry comment has me grinning. "The point is... If you're my cliff, I'll take you every time without looking back."

My chest is so tight I think I'm suffocating. But it can't be, because I'm expanding from the inside out. It's as if I'm going to burst from all of it, and rationally I know it's impossible, but I can't come up with another explanation for the fluttering of my heart, the shivers across my skin.

"But… I was going to come to you," I say when I can manage it. Words are hard when he's looking at me like I'm the answer to everything, but I try. "I needed to do something that mattered, and I thought that's what I was doing by taking over Wicked. I wanted something bigger than me." I think of the kids' music. Music that's now theirs. "But I realized that I don't want to do something bigger than *us*, Jax. I don't want to believe there's *anything* bigger than us. And we can't have an ending, because I'm not done loving you yet." His amber gaze works over mine, his jaw tight with emotion. "I love you more than I thought I could love someone. It's then and it's now and I don't know what will happen tomorrow. But I want to find out with you."

Jax's mouth comes down on mine, and I grip his arms to stay upright.

His kiss is hungry, but more than that, it's home. Not the kind of home that promises safety or security, because nothing can promise that.

The kind that promises compassion, and

love, and kindness, and support. I know he's the man I want to have it all with, the ups and the downs.

When he finally pulls back, he nods to Serena. "I want you to hear something."

She pulls out her phone and hits Play on a song that's familiar and new at once.

"That's Tyler's song." I keep listening. It's different than the version he sent me, because Jax comes in on a verse. Amazement bubbles through me.

"Posted it this morning, with a little Riot Act bump. It's had three million streams since we put it up."

"You recorded this at Wicked?"

"Yup. Wicked's going to have a hard time arguing with the program's success now. It's pulling in ad revenues already."

My head starts to spin and I reach for the wall to steady me.

"You okay?"

"I just signed a deal. Anything recorded by my kids in that studio until eight a.m. today is mine. Exclusively."

His face splits into a grin. "Even better."

"Todd's going to freak," Serena comments. "I don't want to miss this."

With a wink, she disappears down the stairs.

"Who's Todd?" Jax mutters.

My mouth twitches. "No idea. I'm kind of preoccupied."

Jax's eyes darken, and I know what's going through his mind when he says, "me too."

20

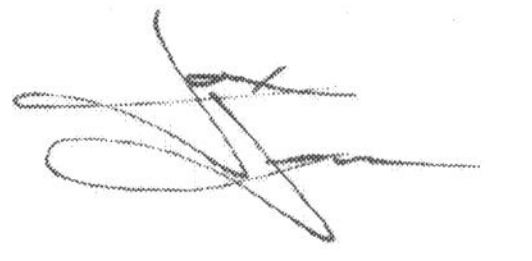

"Hales? You here?" I call from the front hall.

I make my way to the master bedroom to find her rummaging in the closet.

I sneak a look at her cute ass in those jeans as she arranges clothes on hangers. Her hair's up on her head in a bun, and I'm wondering if I can tug it out with one hand or if it'll take two.

"I'm not sure about this 'living in a hotel' thing," she tosses over her shoulder, oblivious to my thoughts.

"You were the one who wanted to sell your house. If you want to buy something new, we can swing it. Unless you'd rather sleep on the bus."

"Definitely not. And since you're keeping your house in Dallas, it seems crazy to have two."

I grin. "Hales? I know people with ten."

She shudders.

"Where's Annie?"

"Out getting ready for dinner. With Tyler."

My interest is officially piqued. Anytime my kid is safe and out of the house and Haley is here, I start to think of some really great ideas.

My gaze drops to the computer on the bed. "You were coding late last night. And again today."

"Mhmm." She turns back to me, lips curved in a knowing smile. "We have this new app—"

I cut her off with a kiss. "You can talk nerdy to me when my tongue's inside you." Without letting her go, I grab her computer and set it on the bedside table none too gently.

Her mouth falls open and I know she's going to protest before she says a word. "Jax, we have an hour before the dinner meeting to talk about growing Big Leap Studio. Serena set it up, and the kids will be there, and—"

"And I'm not spending the hour between

now and then hearing you talk about whatever you're working on with Carter."

I topple her onto the bed and she gasps, laughing. "I do not talk about Carter."

"You're not going to. That's why we're going to have this conversation when my tongue is inside you."

"Good luck with that," she says, but it's breathy. "It's going to take more than your sweet talk, Jax."

"I know."

I strip her shirt over her head, take a second to appreciate the satin of her bra underneath, then reach for my guitar case next to the bed. With a few quick moves, I unhitch the strap from the guitar and hold it out.

Her mouth forms an O. "What are you doing?"

"Wrists out."

"Tell me this isn't ending in a dungeon."

"No dungeons. Just you and me."

She complies, and that alone has me hard. I wrap the soft, wide strap around her wrists and pin them over her head. "Better."

"If you say so." The edge in her voice tells me she's nervous. And excited.

I fucking love making her that way.

There's nothing to prove with this woman, but I've got two years to make up for.

I take my time, skimming my hands over her curves. Unbuttoning her jeans and tugging them down so she's in her underwear. Haley squirms but doesn't move her hands. I hold her hips down on the bed.

Shit, I want to eat her alive.

"What are you doing?" she asks breathlessly.

I strip my shirt over my head, her dark eyes watching every move. "What does it look like?"

My jeans next. And my shorts.

She wets her lips. "I want to touch you."

"No."

Surprise has her blinking. "Jax?"

"Hales. Don't make me tie you to the bed." I shift over her, avoiding touching her flushed skin except where my lips meet her ear. "Because then we definitely won't make dinner."

I couldn't care less about dinner. She's a fucking buffet, and I want to savor every bite. So I do, starting with her lips.

I kiss her, my fingers threading in her hair.

Her arms reach up, but I push them back down so all she can do is writhe against me.

Damn, I like that. My cock twitches against her thigh.

"Tell me how good it feels." I move down to her neck, her shoulders. Light kisses punctuated with the scrape of teeth that make her shiver.

"It would be better if you were inside me," she murmurs.

I suck her hard nipple through the thin lace of her bra, and she jerks against me. "That's the point," I groan.

"Of what?"

"You. Like this."

"That you have to tie me up so we don't both get what we want?"

I grin, because I love how smart and direct she is. Hell, I love everything about her as she lies on my bed, flushed and wanting and so damned real it makes me ache to think of her as mine. "Exactly."

My hands move down, my mouth too, covering every inch of her. Memorizing her body. Until I'm between her thighs, and she moans when my tongue swipes over her clit.

"Jax."

"Uh-huh."

"Some people say don't meet your heroes." She pants the words. "I respectfully disagree."

I chuckle as I move up her body, my gaze moving from her chest to her flushed face to the binding on her hands. I stroke a finger up her arm, and she shivers. I press the strap into the mattress over her head, and her chest rises.

"Me too. I love you, Hales."

"I love you, Jax."

I plunge into her and I'm lost. I pour everything I have, everything I am into her.

Because the thing is, she's already all of it.

EPILOGUE

HALEY

THREE MONTHS LATER

"I can't get it right," I murmur to no one.

My fingers fly over the keyboard, making adjustments. I play the chorus again, closing my eyes and focusing on what's streaming from the headphones.

Nope. DRE had it right the first time. I change it back.

Jax was right. Big Leap is a self-contained studio, and it took me two months to realize it. What's amazing is that starting this fall, we can take it to a school or a library—

anywhere really. But it's still a tour bus. Which means spending too long on it can drive you crazy.

The tapping on my shoulder makes me jump.

"Sorry to scare you," Annie says, her golden eyes lightening in surprise. "My dad's looking for you."

"Oh." I set the headphones around my neck. "And he didn't come himself?"

She has a strange expression on her face. "He's on his way. Just... be nice, okay?"

I'm completely confused as she wanders toward the front of the bus and drops into a seat with her cell phone in her hands. She sneaks a covert look at me.

I shake my head. I love working with kids, but they still stump me sometimes. "Hey, your mom's coming up tomorrow, right?"

She nods. "For the weekend."

Annie still calls Grace her mom and now calls Jax her dad. Is it weird? Sure. Aren't all families?

Grace's been visiting. She and Jax have issues, but they're working through them.

We've been running a test of a summer

program here. Forty kids get time each week in the bus.

The plan is to go back to Dallas in the fall and spend the school year there. We can take the bus to schools across the region, and I can continue to work on projects with Carter, remotely.

Annie's made Jax swear to come back to Philly next summer.

Because in Annie's words: Tyler.

In the past two months, Big Leap's benefited from some news coverage after the single Jax helped produce went gold. That hit is paying for the costs of running the bus, and we worked with the legal team to make sure the kids get compensated through an education fund they can cash in at eighteen if they decide not to pursue school.

It helps that we've put out two more singles, both based on recordings I bought from Wicked, that have been remixed and mastered with the help of my program and Jax's ear. One of them Lita even came in on.

When I told her what happened at Wicked, she dropped an interesting tidbit.

Apparently Todd hit on her when she recorded her last album.

And texted her constantly with some seriously inappropriate propositions after she told him to stop.

Now Wicked's looking for a new head of production.

Motion in the corner of my eye snags my attention and has my stomach flipping as the sexiest guy on the planet climbs the steps.

"You texting Tyler again, squirt?" Jax murmurs to his kid.

"No."

Which means yes.

In two weeks, Annie will be back to school. At least Jax's concern about her finding friends in Philly seems to be ill-founded. Most nights he has to drag her home from hanging out with kids from school and from the studio. Like Tyler.

For all my insistence that he's completely well-intentioned, I see how he looks at her when he's teaching her to play guitar.

Jax thinks Annie will forget him three months after we're back in Dallas.

I say we'll be paying for him to fly in and visit by then.

"Hales?"

I set the headphones on the desk in front of me, leaning back to take him in. I don't even notice what's tucked under his arm, because he's as beautiful as the first time I saw him. His body's hard, lean. Amber eyes that convey way more than they should. A face sculpted from marble, with a mouth made for whispering secrets that make you wet.

He pulls the plexiglass door closed so it's just us here in the studio. "How's the track?"

"It's driving me crazy," I confess. "But I almost have it."

He holds out the hoodie and the frustration melts away.

"You found it!" I gush. "I thought it got lost in the move."

We've been back together for three months, and it's better than I could've imagined. I love working with him. Even if he makes me want to tear my hair out sometimes. He's beyond talented, and any arguments we have are always compensated for by the making up that happens after.

Jax drops onto an amp across from me, shoving the hair back from his face. "Maybe you should put it on."

I take the hoodie, blinking at him.

That's when I realize something's tucked in the front pocket.

I go to pull it out when I notice Jax isn't over me.

He's at eye level.

On one knee.

My throat dries as I pull the box out of the pocket. "Jax..."

He takes it from me, holding it between us. "I never thought I'd find someone who makes me feel like you do. Someone who helped me believe I had a choice again. It doesn't take a crowd to make me feel like a king. All it takes is you."

"*Jax...*"

He shakes his head, but it's the emotion on his face, the conviction on it, that shuts me up. "I don't know what I did to deserve you. But I'm not questioning it anymore."

His gaze drops to the sweatshirt but I can't tear mine from him.

"Hales?"

"Yeah."

"Read the sweatshirt."

"It's been three years," I manage. "I think we've established I have no idea what you put on the damned sweatshirt." But I force my gaze down to it and realize it's embroidered. Black-on-black, nearly invisible, in script that matches his handwriting.

Marry me, Hales.

A gasp from behind me makes us both turn. The plexiglass door is wide open, and two sets of eyes are on us.

Tyler's are amused, poking out from under his hair—which today is green.

Annie's amber eyes are horrified. "You weren't supposed to propose on the bus!"

"Why not?" Jax demands.

"It's not every girl's dream!"

"You have dreams of getting proposed to?" Tyler asks. Annie flushes, but Jax misses it. His attention is back on me.

"Hales, I'll ask you anywhere you want. Every day for the rest of our lives. We need to have more kids. Cuz Annie's old enough to babysit, so it's cheap from here on in."

"I heard that!" Annie gushes, then gasps. "Dad, she *still* didn't answer."

"Good point." Jax shifts back on his heels, eyes intent on mine. He opens the box and lifts the ring.

It's simple. One diamond in the center, blinking in the light from the window.

"Your move, Hales."

I bite the side of my cheek as emotions rush through me.

Annie sighs. "Come on, Haley, don't do this to him."

"What am I supposed to say?"

He's starting to look uncomfortable. "Yes would be a start."

I pretend to consider it. "Well. I guess I'd better." I lower my voice so only he can hear. "I mean, you're Jax fucking Jamieson."

Jax's grin splits his face, and even before he slips the ring on my finger, I know I've done something right.

EPILOGUE

"I'm not sure why you wanted to drop me off. I have a car."

I follow Haley through the carpeted halls of the campus building. "I felt like it."

She peers through a doorway. "Hey, Carter."

"Haley." He comes into view.

Surrounded by books and computers and awards, Dr. Christopher Carter is shorter than I expected.

Which makes me inordinately happy.

His gaze drops, and he makes a noise in his throat. "You got engaged?"

"Last week. We're moving to Dallas in the fall. Carter, this is Jax."

I step up next to her, and he raises a brow.

"Jax. As in Jax Jamieson," he says.

I grin. "Yeah. You've heard of me, Connor?"

"Carter."

"Right." I wrap my arm around her waist.

She checks her phone. "So I sent you the latest for our meeting today. Did you get the code?"

"Yeah." But that blue gaze is squarely on me, as though he's sizing me up.

Bring it.

"Does your boyfriend want to stay?"

"Fiancé. But he's right, I gotta go, Hales. Shooting a clothing ad spot." I pat my rock-hard abs through my shirt. "It's hard to keep in shape after thirty, right? But they keep calling."

"Uh-huh." The other man shoves his hands in the pockets of his douchey trousers.

"See you tonight." I turn to Haley, tugging on her waist to bring her lips up to mine.

Her eyebrows shoot up, but she lets me kiss her.

At first.

Then she's totally into it. She knows it's

bullshit, but she can't stop her fingers from digging into my biceps. Just like I can't stop the way holding her has blood rushing to my cock.

Before the situation can get too far out of control, I pull back.

She's blinking and I'm a little dizzy too, but I keep it together.

Haley's lips curve like she's onto me, but she stifles a snort. "See you, Jax."

"Later, Hales." I turn for the door.

"Yeah. See you, Jax."

I lift a hand over my head. "See ya, Connor."

I shove my hands in my pockets and whistle as I start down the hallway.

Thanks for reading *Wicked Girl*! I hope you loved reading Jax and Haley's story as much as I loved writing it.

If you're not ready to give them up, you can now read Jax and Haley's wedding story in *Forever Wicked!*

Sign up for Piper Lawson's newsletter to get free books, exclusive deals and more. You'll instantly receive an exclusive Jax and Haley anniversary bonus chapter! https://claims.prolificworks.com/free/XnsF5IyN

As an indie author, I sincerely appreciate you reading and helping spread the word!

If you loved *Wicked Girl*, please consider leaving a quick review. Reviews help readers like you find books they'll love.

NEXT UP FOR JAX AND HALEY...

Read a short excerpt below

CHAPTER ONE

Haley

Five days until the wedding

There's nothing like a man on his knees.

Naked to the waist, eyes closed.

Especially when that man is Jax Jamieson and he's on his knees for me.

"I wonder if you taste as good as I remember."

The biggest rock star in a generation yanks my skirt up around my hips, his half-lidded eyes locking on their target between my thighs.

My greedy gaze roams his gorgeous face and tight jaw, his sculpted shoulders and chest and abs.

It still blows my mind that he's mine.

The damp air in the garage is nothing compared to the dampness between my legs right now.

"It hasn't been that long," I protest breathily, my hands kneading his shoulders.

"No man should be without his wife for a month before their wedding."

"It's not fair to him?"

"It's not fair to her."

Our plan to sell my father's house in Philadelphia before moving the last of my, and his, belongings to Jax's mansion in Dallas with time to spare before the wedding had seemed foolproof.

Still, some emergency roadblocks complicated the sale, meaning I'd had to spend the last month in Philly while Jax and Annie were here in Dallas because of Annie's school and a promotional gig Jax had committed to.

Now with less than a week until the wedding, we're still tripping over moving boxes from Philly while our friends and loved ones are descending on Dallas.

Did I mention we haven't gotten a moment alone together since I got back?

Jax's hands skim up my thighs, thumbs grazing so close to where I need him.

"Wider." That voice the world has paid millions to hear is commanding, and right now, it's commanding me.

My body tries to comply, desperate to give him access to what he wants—what we want—but my foot is blocked by something hard.

I try to lift my leg higher, to catch the top of the cardboard moving box, but there's another stacked on top of it and my foot slides back down.

On a growl, Jax grabs my hips and turns me without even rising. My shoulder blades hit a metal shelf, and I suck in a breath, but I manage to widen my stance a few inches.

Each pore on my body, each fiber of my being, insists that Jax's tongue between my thighs will fix every ache I own.

He's hovering millimeters from where I need him. Vibration tingles through my body, radiating down my legs, to my fingertips that grab his shoulders for balance. The muscles there ripple, making the tattoos down his bicep and forearm jump in time to my heartbeat.

"Tell me how much you missed me," he rasps.

I take a moment to appreciate Jax's fiery amber eyes, the cocky tilt of his full mouth, the determined line of his jaw.

"I might have thought of you once or twice," I say saucily because I take my job of managing his enormous ego seriously. "I also thought about seating charts and flowers and whether we should add a sorbet to dessert."

He hooks a finger in the panel of my panties, already soaked, and drags it to the side. His breath on me has me trembling.

Though I hadn't been looking forward to spending time away from Jax, I'd reasoned it would be possible. I spent twenty-one years without him; a few weeks wouldn't kill me.

Apparently, that was optimistic. Because in those twenty-one years, I hadn't gotten used to his commanding presence at my side and in my bed like I have in the year we've been engaged.

It was like growing up without the sun only

to be forced back underground the moment you experienced its warmth.

During my month alone in Philly, I learned phone sex does less to resolve tension than to escalate it. And getting myself off to the memory of my fiancé's touch, his lips, his cock, is a poor substitute for the real thing.

"The only dessert you thought of is me eating this pussy until you're begging me to stop."

His finger slides against my entrance. *Not fair.*

He teases me until I moan.

"Yes," I whisper.

But instead of devouring me like I want him to, Jax pulls back.

"We're going upstairs." His breath is unsteady. "I'm going to lock the door. And fuck my future wife until she swears to never leave me again."

His words have me boneless, but even though I want to float away on a wave of desire, the logical part of my brain won't leave.

"I can't take this afternoon off," I manage. "I have a dress appointment, then I need to find somewhere quiet to review an app for Carter and... oh—"

Jax's finger flicks my clit hard enough that I jump.

"Don't say his name when I'm fucking you." His harsh edge is dulled by the wave of pleasure radiating from my core as his fingers continue to caress my opening.

"You're not fucking me. You're teasing me." My hands flex in his hair as need to assert myself twines with longing, the ever-present temptation to ignore the world and say yes to anything this man could ask of me. "And I can't drop work for this entire week on account of the wedding."

"I don't want you to drop work for a week. I want you to drop it for two."

His fingers press inside me as if to prove a point, and this time, I do moan. It's impossible to reconcile the sudden fullness in me with the need for more as my hips arch against his hand.

"Next week it'll be you and me on a beach in Bali, and every sweet inch of this"—his thumb rubs a circle over my clit, and I hiccup at the bolt of desire that shocks me—"is mine until I say so."

Bali. It's like a prayer. Something to cling to when it's all too much.

Sand.

Solitude.

Me and the man I love and zero interruptions.

I'd figured once everything in Philly was finalized and my belongings were here, the actual wedding would be straightforward, but since the moment invitations went out more than six months ago, congratulations and gifts have poured in by the hundreds.

The biggest wedding of the decade—which has nothing to do with me and everything to do with the fact that I'm marrying Jax Jamieson—has gone from "massive" to "Richter scale registering," a storm that's built its own velocity and is threatening to destroy everything in its path.

But Jax's mouth lowers between my thighs, and I know the desperate ache in me is about to resolve.

"Promise you're mine for the next two weeks," he murmurs against my needy skin, "and I'll make you come so hard they'll hear you back in Philly."

The vibration from Jax's mouth has me clutching the shelf behind me, fingers slipping on the cold metal as I swallow a moan. But the feel of his soft hair in my fingers, his hot mouth between my thighs, his commanding grip on my ass, tears at my control. "*Yes.*"

"Fuck, I love hearing you say that word. Almost makes up for all the times you told me no."

White-hot pleasure descends on me as his mouth finally claims me.

My fingers grasp for the shelf, and this time it tips forward—just a few inches, but enough to send something rolling off the front.

"Jax, look out!" I startle out of my haze fast enough grab the can of paint as it drops through the air, a millisecond before it lands on his beautiful face.

The shock of what nearly happened rips through the arousal, leaving me shaking with adrenaline.

My almost-husband smirks. "We're not even married yet, and you're trying to kill me?"

I set the can on the floor, shaking off the

horror from the sight of it falling toward Jax. "I don't want to kill you," I pant. "I'd miss your mouth too much."

Jax straightens, eyes glowing as he brushes an impatient thumb down my cheek. "I miss every part of you, Hales, and we're both right here."

My heart melts as I take in the man I love, the one I still can't believe I'm marrying in a few days.

His dirty words have me aching again. He trails a finger down my stomach, making my breath hitch before it dips between my thighs.

"Haley! Jax! I know what you're doing in there," a voice shouts through the closed door to the house.

I squeeze my eyes shut as Jax's hand stills, willing us both to block out the sound.

When nothing comes after one heartbeat, two, five, I think I've succeeded.

Until a pounding comes at the door.

"Haley, you have a dress fitting in thirty minutes, and there's an accident in town! We need to leave now."

Alarm breaks through my sex-induced

haze. "Shit! I thought it wasn't for another hour and a half."

"I won't be done with you in thirty minutes. But if they want to come to the house, I can work under the dress."

My thighs press together at his seductive promise.

"I'm coming in," Serena threatens, separated from us by only a few inches of wood.

My face drains of blood.

"Fucking hell." Jax withdraws from my body, and I bite my lip to stop from complaining. He starts toward the door, fury in every taut muscle.

"Jax! Stop it." I lunge, hooking two fingers in the waist of his jeans and wincing as they nearly dislocate. I manage to get between him and the door without tripping over myself, and I work my clothes back into place between words. "Don't bite Serena's head off. It's not her fault."

Frustration and concern color the amber eyes I love. "Let's elope. I'll have a charter on the tarmac in an hour."

My lips curve into a trembling smile. "We

wanted to do this right, remember? I wanted our friends. You wanted it in Dallas..."

Reluctant hands help me straighten my ruined underwear and wrinkled skirt as he drops his forehead to mine.

"Fine, but I'm going to make you come once for every night we spent apart," he vows. "You're getting at least a week of orgasms tonight."

He presses his mouth to mine in a hard kiss that's a reminder of what we were just doing and that the patience he's exhibiting right now is a gift.

"What're you doing this afternoon?" I ask. "Helping Brick taste-test the cake? Or arranging carbon offsets for all the guests with Kyle?"

"Something better." His eyes gleam as if he's holding a secret over my head simply to punish me.

It's working.

I'm dying to know, but hearing my name shouted through the door again pulls my attention away.

"This isn't over. Tonight." He presses my

hand against the bulge in his jeans that has me lusting after him even more.

With a last look that does nothing to cool my insides, he grabs his shirt off the floor, tugs it over his head, and starts for the door.

End of Sample

To continue reading, be sure to pick up *Forever Wicked* at your favorite retailer.

WHY I WROTE "WICKED"

Confession: I've always wanted to write a rock star romance.

But I knew if I did it (1) it probably wouldn't feel like any other rock star romance out there, (2) it couldn't be about the bougie lifestyle, it had to be about basic human crap we all deal with, (3) it needed a quirky heroine who was, in the words of one of my readers, 'flawed but not broken'.

I planned it out in 3 parts over more than 2 years because I didn't want to focus only on the music, or the family drama, or the tour. I wanted to show the ups and downs of Haley and Jax's life. I wanted this book to be about how at the end of the day, we get to make our own choices, even when it feels like we don't.

That beautiful truth is something I can write books about all day long.

We get to decide how we think, how we feel, how we act. And we can't control the universe, but we control who our friends are, how we spend our time, whether we make ourselves vulnerable, and the stories we tell about our lives. The parts we've lived, and the parts yet to come.

It also means we don't have to have a 'perfect' past, we don't need to be famous, or rich, we just need to decide how we want to show up every moment of every day.

Thank you for spending part of your day with Jax and Haley.

XX,
Piper

P.S. Think other romance readers might enjoy Wicked? Please consider leaving a review for *Wicked Girl* (or the Wicked series)! Reviews help readers find books, and you could help someone you've never met find their next read. Which is kind of awesome, if you think about it.

BOOKS BY PIPER LAWSON

FOR A FULL LIST PLEASE GO TO

PIPERLAWSONBOOKS.COM/BOOKS

OFF-LIMITS SERIES

Turns out the beautiful man from the club is my new professor... But he wasn't when he kissed me.

Off-Limits is a forbidden age gap college romance series. Find out what happens when the beautiful man from the club is Olivia's hot new professor.

WICKED SERIES

Rockstars don't chase college students. But Jax Jamieson never followed the rules.

Wicked is a new adult rock star series full of nerdy girls, hot rock stars, pet skunks, and ensemble casts you'll want to be friends with forever.

RIVALS SERIES

At seventeen, I offered Tyler Adams my home, my life, my heart. He stole them all.

Rivals is an angsty new adult series. Fans of forbidden romance, enemies to lovers, friends to lovers, and rock star romance will love these books.

ENEMIES SERIES

I sold my soul to a man I hate. Now, he owns me.

Enemies is an enthralling, explosive romance about an American DJ and a British billionaire. If you like wealthy, royal alpha males, enemies to lovers, travel or sexy romance, this series is for you!

TRAVESTY SERIES

My best friend's brother grew up. Hot.

Travesty is a steamy romance series following best friends who start a fashion label from NYC to LA. It contains best friends brother, second chances, enemies to lovers, opposites attract and friends to lovers stories. If you like sexy, sassy romances, you'll love this series.

PLAY SERIES

I know what I want. It's not Max Donovan. To hell with his money, his gaming empire, and his joystick.

Play is an addictive series of standalone romances with slow burn tension, delicious banter, office romance and unforgettable characters. If you like smart, quirky, steamy enemies-to-lovers, contemporary romance, you'll love Play.

MODERN ROMANCE SERIES

When your rich, handsome best friend asks you to be his fake girlfriend? Say no.

Modern Romance is a smart, sexy series of contemporary romances following a set of female friends running a relationship marketing company in NYC. If you enjoy hot guys who treat their families like gold, fun antics, dirty talk, real characters, steamy scenes, badass heroines and smart banter, you'll love the Modern Romance series.

ABOUT THE AUTHOR

Piper Lawson is a WSJ and USA Today bestselling author of smart and steamy romance.

She writes women who follow their dreams, best friends who know your dirty secrets and love you anyway, and complex heroes you'll fall hard for.

Piper lives in Canada with her tall and brilliant husband. She's a sucker for dark eyes, dark coffee, and dark chocolate.

For a complete reading list, visit www.piperlawsonbooks.com/books

Subscribe to Piper's VIP email list www.piperlawsonbooks.com/subscribe

amazon.com/author/piperlawson
bookbub.com/authors/piper-lawson
instagram.com/piperlawsonbooks
facebook.com/piperlawsonbooks
goodreads.com/piperlawson

THANK YOUS

This book wouldn't have happened without the support of my awesome advance team and reader group (ladies - thank you for the support, nail biting, and patiently rocking in the corner while I finished part 3). Pam and Renate, thank you for your eagle eyes! Nothing gets by you. Mandee, thank you for creating Jax's rock star-worthy signature, Jax is at least 20% more badass now. Natasha, you are the most amazing designer, thank you for letting me tweak this until we got it just right. Lindee, I couldn't imagine better photography to inspire my books. Cassie and Devon, thank you for questioning, polishing, and pointing out I meant to say IV chord, not iV chord. Danielle, thank you for the amazing promo graphics, and generally helping me stay organized and making sure I don't release new books in a vacuum. Plus of course Mr. L, the world's best beta reader and the guy who makes sure my world doesn't break while I'm sequestered in my writing cave. Thank you all from the bottom of my heart.

Manufactured by Amazon.ca
Bolton, ON